QUINN: COWBOY RISK

THE KAVANAGH BROTHERS BOOK TWO

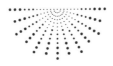

KATHLEEN BALL

I dedicate this to all the members of my Facebook Kathleen Ball Western Romance Readers group.
And as always to Bruce, Steven, Colt, Clara and Mavis because I love them.

CHAPTER ONE

*Q*uinn Kavanagh kicked a stone out of his way. It sailed in a low arc and landed to the side of the track on the dust-dry ground. Sweat stung his eyes, and he took off his hat and mopped at his forehead with his sleeve. He fought an urge to lift his gaze skyward. If he looked at the sun one more time, he'd end up sunblind. Except for the scuffle of footfalls on parched earth, they walked in silence. Even the insects and birds had the good sense to get out of the beating sun. His paint, Bandit plodded along behind him, favoring his front left foot. It was sluggish going as the sun continued its relentless glare and more sweat trickled down Quinn's soaked back.

Of all the places to live, why Texas? Sure, it was a great state, but that sun.

All around him, as far as the eye could see, scrub brush, cracked earth, and more scrub brush. His current situation was his own fault. It had been his choice to leave home. He needed time alone to get his head right. He'd discovered the family ranch belonged to his brother Teagan and *only* Teagan. The sweat and blood of all the Kavanaghs had built the ranch, yet their father had left it all to Teagan. It was just too hard to swallow.

His heart felt shredded as it always did when he thought of home. Quinn and his other eight brothers had thought they had inherited equal shares. Why the pretense? That was what galled him the most. He and Teagan had been close, very close.

He sighed. That was the past, and who knew what was around the next bend? And did it really matter? Anything but scorching sun and gritty dust all day would suit him. He was still young, but he felt much older, ever since fighting in the War Between the States. It had aged his soul something fierce, and there were scars inside and out that would never heal.

His paint snorted and bobbed his head, sniffing the air.

Quinn glanced over his shoulder. "Don't worry, Bandit, I can smell water too. Probably just over this here mound."

The crack of a gunshot not too far off broke the silence. Bandit tried to pull away. Quinn gripped the reins and grabbed his rifle. He jumped down and snatched his saddle bags before he let Bandit go. He wouldn't go too far. Inching up the hill, Quinn saw an old homestead, a small lake, and what appeared to be a woman with a rifle standing on the porch of the house with three men pointing guns at her.

The shot had most likely come from her, but it didn't look as though it had scared the men off. He was behind the men and he calculated if he could sneak up on them before they turned around. There was a decent sized boulder, a water trough, and a wagon to use as cover if needed.

He made sure his guns were loaded and ready. Then he put shotgun shells into his pocket before he eased down the hill. He could tell by the small jerk of the woman's head, she'd seen him. Giving a quick shake of his head, he touched a finger to his lips, warning her to be quiet. She didn't give him away. Hopefully she was the type that could be counted on. She waited until he reached the boulder before she shot the ground in front of the men and ran into the house. She managed to close the door before they stormed it.

Quinn watched them for a moment and when it looked as though they were going to shoot at the house, he shot into the ground behind them. They whipped around fast, scanning the area, seeking the shooter. They fanned out a bit and cautiously walked away from the house.

Another shot rang out, and one of the men was down. It must have been the woman. The men turned toward the house and Quinn didn't have much choice when one man put the butt of his rifle against his shoulder.

Quinn shot him in the arm and the rifle dropped. The third man ran to his horse, jumped on and galloped away. Slowly Quinn approached the house when the woman came out again. "Hold it right there!"

"I mean no harm, ma'am."

"I'll be the judge of that. What are you doing here?" She proceeded down the porch steps and kicked the man who'd been shot in the leg.

He howled.

"That'll teach you to bully women." She settled a cool glare on Quinn, one eyebrow raised waiting for him to explain himself.

"I thought there might be water this way, and my horse needed water. I want to rest him a bit. I can just keep going if that suits you better." He had his six-shooter in his hand with his finger on the trigger.

"Mister you don't have a horse." She angled her head in challenge as she stared at him. "You just happen to be here when these here men tried to kill me?"

"I'm not looking for trouble. In fact, I'm looking for a place where I can find a bit of peace."

She squinted. "In the war, wasn't you?"

"Yes, ma'am."

"What side?"

He had a fifty-fifty chance of giving the right answer. Not all who now lived in Texas backed the Confederacy. He shrugged and settled on telling the truth. "I'm a Rebel through and through."

"Hmm. Not everyone admits to being on the losing side."

"We didn't lose, we just didn't win. This time." He'd walked closer as he talked. She was younger than he thought. Where were her folks? Was she even sixteen? He caught a flash of her blue eyes and noted the riot of her blond hair that might have been combed a few days ago. It didn't take away from her beauty.

She smiled. "Now if you only had a horse, I'd think you trustworthy."

"Bandit's coming this way, isn't he?"

She nodded.

"Could someone get this bullet out of my leg before I die?" the man on the ground asked.

"If you're lucky, I'll take it out after you die. I need every bullet I have."

The injured man's eyes widened. "Why would that make me lucky?"

"I'm not a gentle woman with a light touch. I'm more of a stick a knife in and keep cutting until I find the bullet type of woman."

The man cringed, from pain or fear, Quinn couldn't tell which.

She stepped forward and took his firearms away along with those of the dead man and then stacked them on the porch. She shot Quinn a glance. "I have a small barn in back, if you want to tend your horse." She nodded toward the lake. "He's a healthy drinker."

Quinn nodded his thanks as he took the reins and led Bandit to the back. The barn was adequate. He opened a stall door and jumped back, reeling in surprise to see a bunch of children hiding inside, eyes wide with fear.

"Howdy," he said with a smile. "I thought maybe Bandit here could rest in this stall, but I can see it's taken." He closed the door and went to the next stall. It was empty. The children didn't make one peep. It was unsettling.

"It's safe to come out my little lambs. Come now, I'll make up something to eat."

The shuffling of feet and the rustle of clothing told Quinn the children were leaving. But he was startled when the woman stuck her head in the stall. "Mister, could you drag the dead body out to those rocks to the west? I don't want the children to see him. Then I'll help you bring the other one into the barn here. If he lives, he lives… if not, it's to the rock pile."

If she hadn't been staring waiting for an answer, he would have been speechless. He spread his hands and offered a nod. "I… can do that."

She smiled. "I'm Heaven Burke, and you are?"

He tipped his hat. "Quinn Kavanagh. It's a pleasure, Miss Burke."

"Heaven, please. My father called me his little piece of Heaven on Earth."

She'd appear angelic if it wasn't for the rifle. Her honey-blond hair looked soft and silky even though it was a mess. Her blue eyes were a no-nonsense steel blue, though, cold and resolute.

"I'll see you inside." Her voice had a hard edge to it as though to warn him she'd be armed.

He finished with Bandit, moved the dead man to the rock pile and dragged the other man into the barn. Thankfully the wounded man had passed out and didn't put up a fight.

Quinn took his guns and saddlebags with him as he walked into the house. It was bigger than it looked, and all the children had a place at the table.

"Make yourself comfortable, Quinn. There's always plenty of room at my table."

He removed his hat and hung it on a peg near the door and then laid his saddlebags on the floor. He walked to the fireplace and set his firearms up on the mantel so the children couldn't reach them. Then he went to the table and grinned. "I'm Quinn."

"This is Tim and Daisy." She pointed to two of the children closest to her. "They're mine. And then we have Joshua, Manuel, and Peter, who are visiting for a while."

Quinn smiled at fair-haired Tim and Daisy and at the three black boys, Joshua, Manuel, and Peter. "Nice to meet you." He sat on an empty chair at the table and helped himself to a ham sandwich. He laughed as the children nudged each other and made faces at one another.

After the noon meal Heaven put Daisy down for a nap and had the boys play quietly. She was sweet and gentle with the children. It warmed his heart to observe it. After a fashion, she took a seat across from him.

"I bet you're wondering about everything around here." She gestured to their surroundings. "I take in Negro children who have nowhere to go. They're always boys. I'm part of a network that either finds the children's parents or a decent home. It's not a popular concept. I guess people would rather the children die in this part of Texas. The men today were here to take the children. I wish they'd just mind their own business and let us be."

"What were they going to do with them?"

Tears moistened her eyes. "Sell them."

He reeled backward in his seat. "To who? Everyone knows slavery is over."

"They are sold as laborers. There are still crops to be picked. They are workers who don't get paid and can't leave. You see their pay goes to room, board, clothing, and whatever else they may need. Before they know it, they owe much more than they make, and they can't leave while owing money. I think they sell girls over the border in Mexico. But girls always get grabbed up before I get a chance to rescue them."

His gut clenched. "Where do you find these children?"

"Usually walking, looking for water. They keep the strong ones and let the weaker ones go. But they don't want me interfering." She stared at the table.

"Where's your husband?"

"They hauled him off and killed him when they found out he was actively riding out looking for the boys. They took the boys at the time too."

Anger filled him. "When was this?"

"Well over a year ago." Her voice was full of despair.

He couldn't help but look at her swollen belly. She was carrying, but that wasn't his business. "That ain't right. What about the law?"

A wry smile twisted her lips. "They *are* the law around here. They'll be back in force when they find out one of their men was killed and the other injured. I figure we have about a half hour left before they come. You'd best get going." She glanced up and gave him a sad smile while she laid her hands protectively over her unborn babe.

Pounding hoofbeats rumbled on the ground outside. Heaven gasped and stared at the door, wide-eyed. That sounded like a lot of horses riding toward them.

"I don't think we have that half hour." Quinn got up and peeked out the window. He felt her right behind him.

She released a relieved sigh. "Boys get ready! Joshua,

Manuel, and Peter, the good men are here to take you to safe homes."

The three darker-skinned boys turned and stared at her with fright in their eyes.

She went to them and kneeled. "Listen my sweets, I trust these men. There will be good, safe homes where no one will sell you. I'm hoping they can find your parents. Don't be scared." She took four peppermint stick candies out of her apron pocket and handed one to each boy, including her own son. Each boy received a tight hug. Then she went into one of the bedrooms and came back with three bundles of clothes. "These belong to you. Be good now." Heaven led them outside and smiled as each boy was put on a horse with a rider. She watched until they were out of sight and then tears poured down her face.

CHAPTER TWO

"I was so hoping they'd be gone before the men came. They would have taken them for sure. I think one day they might even kill me. I can't turn children away, and word is out that this is a safe house." She glanced up at Quinn. "You might as well go. No sense you getting caught up in my troubles. It was nice to meet you." He was so tall and handsome. If only she could lean against him. Just for a moment. She needed strength. God was with her, of course, and she had the utmost faith that He was always there. It was just hard.

He was already shaking his head. "I'm not leaving. I *was* looking for peace but protecting you and your children is much more important. That is… if you don't mind my staying for a bit."

His big blue eyes held her gaze as he waited for her answer.

Relief washed over her, and she nodded. "I could use a bit of help, and I'd be grateful for a few days of it." He'd best realize he was sleeping on the floor. She might be a widow but that didn't mean she made free with her affections. More hoofbeats thundered outside. She'd make sure he understood after the townsmen left.

"They're coming."

"Get your daughter and son somewhere low and safe."

She nodded and ran to get Tim into the bedroom with Daisy. When she came back, she was surprised to see three rifles in three different places with extra shells on the floor. Two of the rifles were hers.

"I'll need you to load the rifles as quickly as you can. Stay low. I want them to think more than one man is in here. Don't make a sound. I'm going to tell them you and your children left. Shoot your gun occasionally when I'm at a different window. We need to keep them guessing."

For just a moment, she stared, not moving. She was putting a lot of trust in a stranger and that wasn't like her. But as the sound of men's voices reached her ears, she nodded and sat on the floor near the first window, waiting.

"Heaven Burke, get out here! You just never learn, do you? It's time for another lesson!" yelled a man in a red shirt named Marsh Down, the leader.

She started to gasp, but she quickly put her hand over her mouth. Quinn sent her a questioning glance, but she looked away.

The men built a fire in the yard. Did they plan to burn her at the stake? Maybe they were going to burn the house down. Her hands shook. Then she saw them put a branding iron in the fire and fear coursed through her. They intended to use it on her. She'd heard of them doing it before but never on a white woman.

"Don't worry," Quinn whispered.

She nodded and swallowed hard, but she didn't believe him. What if they went after her children or hurt the baby she carried? It unnerved her.

A rock slammed against the door, hard.

"Come on out, Heaven! It's time you learned once and for all to stop helping Negroes."

Quinn put his finger to his lips. "What's going on out there? Who are you? What do you want?"

"We're here for Heaven Burke," hollered Marsh Down. "She broke the rules, and now she has to be punished."

A chill raced down her spine.

"I'm afraid you won't find her here," Quinn called back. "I bought this ranch. She left, took on outa here with a passel o' kids."

"Well now," Marsh yelled. "I sent three men here this morning and only one came back with a story about a man with no horse. She was here then."

"Yes, she was. But not for long. I helped her drag one man to the rock pile, and there's another in the barn. Don't know and don't care whether or not he's dead. Men came for the boys, and she wouldn't let them take 'em. Sold me the place right on the spot." He chuckled. "Got myself a good deal too."

The silence from outside nearly undid her. Heaven risked a careful glance out the window.

Marsh, Dick, and Rupert were all whispering to each other. Another man she didn't recognize was on his way to the barn.

"Well..." Marsh took the branding iron out of the fire and studied the end. "If you see the wench, tell her I'm going to kill her."

Not if she killed him first! Heaven lunged for the door, but Quinn tackled her and slapped a hand over her mouth. "I'll be sure to tell her!"

SHE STRUGGLED AGAINST HIS HOLD, but he tightened his grasp and gave her a little shake.

"Are you trying to get us killed?" he hissed.

More calls came from outside, and then the horses thundered away from the house.

Slowly Quinn eased away as it struck him that he had just thrown a pregnant woman to the hard floor. He sat next to her and stared. She blinked at him. Blinking was good wasn't it?

Reaching out he touched her stomach. "Did I hurt you or the baby?" His throat felt dry. What if he had harmed the baby?

She tried to sit up, and he assisted her. "Do you need a cup of water? Do you think you can stand?"

"I'm fine, really. You were trying to keep me safe. It's been a long time since anyone did that." She stood and brushed off her dress. "Just be gentler next time," she said unruffled.

Quinn helped her into a chair, peered out the window to be sure the men were gone, and then poured Heaven a cup of water.

"Thank you." She took a sip. "Let Tim and Daisy know they can come out. If Daisy is sleeping leave her be."

He opened the bedroom door and Tim flew at him and wrapped his little arms around Quinn's waist. Quinn picked him up and brought him to Heaven. He went back into the bedroom and there was Daisy lying on a quilt on the floor with her thumb in her mouth. How precious she looked with wisps of blond curls around her head. He bent down to lift her onto the bed when her eyes flew open. A shriek that could have wakened all of Texas came out of the little girl's mouth. He startled.

"I'm not going to hurt you, I was just going to put you on the bed."

Daisy gave him a glare that would have made a wolf back away.

Heaven was in the room in an instant, and she hurriedly

scooped up Daisy. She gave Quinn a saucy grin while humor danced in her eyes. "I told you to leave her." She chuckled as she left the room.

Laughter? That tiny girl's shriek had near terrified him, and it was funny? He walked back out and Heaven held Daisy on her lap while she had an arm around Tim. Somehow, he'd need to get them away from here.

"I saw a wagon out back. I think we should pack up. It's not safe for you here."

"The children know to come here to be safe. I can't abandon them."

"I respect you for what you've been doing, but my motto has always been live to fight another day. You know as well as I they'll be back. You need to protect the ones you have." He stared into her eyes. They were full of doubt. "I don't have a solution for the boys wandering out there looking for this house. But it does no good if they…" He gazed at the children. "I really think packing up to leave will be best."

Her eyes filled, and she gave him a forlorn smile. "You're right."

"I'll help you pack. I saw a few crates in the barn. Those horses you have, do they know how to pull a wagon?"

"It's been a while, but they do. You'll find everything you need in the barn."

He nodded. "I'd like to leave in a few hours."

Her teary eyes widened and then she nodded hesitantly as she stood and set Daisy on the chair.

He felt awful, but it was imperative she got away from those men before they brought a whole posse.

"I'll get the crates." He left the house and entered the barn. Just as he expected, the wounded man was gone.

CHAPTER THREE

Quinn walked ahead, leading the horses in the moonlight. Heaven had packed quickly and never once complained. She had taken the children to their father's grave, and there were tears in her eyes when they returned to the wagon. But she'd wiped them away and then made it seem like a great adventure for the children. She had many qualities to admire. Maybe most important, she didn't ask too many questions.

He didn't know what to do with them except bring them to the Kavanagh ranch. Teagan's ranch, he thought with a bitter taste in his mouth. But there was no other choice. He'd have to go an around-about way, erase tracks and then make false trails. He didn't trust those men one bit and he had no intention of having his neck stretched. He stopped the wagon in a grove of trees and then untied Bandit from the back of the wagon. "I'll be back soon. I want to make sure we aren't being followed. You might as well eat, but no fire." He had the urge to kiss her cheek and that unnerved him. He never wanted urges or desire again.

When Heaven's weathered house came into his sight, he

instantly spotted a man coming out. He was about average height, but with a bandana covering the bottom half of his face, there was no way to identify him. Quinn's hand itched to pull his gun and shoot the man, but he kept out of sight, watching until he left.

When he was certain no one else remained on the ranch, Quinn worked quickly and covered their tracks the best he could. Hopefully, no one had noticed them heading out already. His thoughts drifted to his urge to shoot the intruder. Why would he want to kill that man? He'd never wanted to pull the trigger before. He'd seen enough killing in the war. He didn't have the stomach for it or for any conflict. And here he was right in the middle of trouble. He clenched his teeth. At least he wouldn't get attached to the family. His heart had gone cold years ago, and those types of emotions were dead. His heart had been sealed off the day he discovered the woman he loved had lied to him. She'd used a fake name and then disappeared and couldn't be found.

His brother Teagan often said he didn't smile anymore. That was true. There was nothing to smile about. His body bore the scars of the war, and his heart was mangled by love. He'd often wished he had died on the battlefield. But he hadn't. Instead, he died over and over again, every day when he saw his hideous scars and thought of the deceptive woman he'd loved. He willed it all to stop, the emotions, the reminders... but they were there every morning when he awoke, and he dreaded going to sleep knowing the dawning of the next day would bring unbearable grief.

He'd thrown all his energy into making the Kavanagh ranch the best in Texas, and he'd recently been blindsided when he'd found out he didn't own a stake in the operation. He'd had to leave. He hadn't planned to go back, but Heaven needed a place that was safe. So they'd skirt the towns and hope they weren't seen.

He rubbed his hand over his weary face. The night was escaping, and he had to get back to the wagon. He didn't want Heaven and her children afraid. He'd have to find a way for those wandering boys to get to safety.

The leather of his saddle creaked as he dismounted. He took the reins and led Bandit into the camp. The children were asleep with their heads on Heaven's lap. She tilted her head back until their gazes met. He wasn't prepared for the blissful smile she gave him. It coursed through him and scared him.

Tamping down his feelings, he led Bandit away to take care of him.

HE DIFFERED from any man she'd ever met. She never once saw him look at her in any way but respectful. He didn't make false promises, at least so far. It was if he thought of her and the children as some responsibility that he needed to shoulder. His eyes were troubled.

Surely he knew how babies were made and he could count. She'd been honest about when her husband had died. Yet he hadn't asked who the father of the baby was or appeared disgusted when he asked if the baby was hurt when he pushed her to safety. He probably didn't welcome questions about himself, so perhaps that meant he understood there would be things she didn't want to speak of. So far, she trusted him, and she could only hope her instincts were correct.

He sat and leaned against his saddle he'd placed near her. He seemed exhausted.

Heaven immediately handed him some bread and cheese.

"I'm grateful." He glanced at her and then gazed out into the darkness.

"I'm grateful too. The children went right to sleep after they ate."

"I'll roll a couple of oil cloths under the wagon and carry them to bed. It has been a long day. I wasn't sure we'd be alive yet, here we are."

He ate and then walked to the back of the wagon. He grabbed what she suspected were the oil cloths. After he had them under the wagon, he put the quilt from her bed on top of the cloth and then set quilts in a pile to cover them.

She smiled appreciatively when he lifted Tim and carefully laid him on the quilt and then put another quilt over him. He certainly was a gentle man. When he came back for Daisy, she fussed but he held her to him, and she put her head on his shoulder and went back to sleep.

Tears spilled down her face. She missed David still. He used to carry Daisy in much the same fashion. Hastily she wiped away her tears and stood. Tomorrow promised to be a long tiring day.

"Going to bed?" he asked softly.

"Yes. Thank you for everything." She wished she had a smile to give.

"I'll see you in the morning. We'll go for a while then stop to make coffee if no one is following us. I hate thinking people in this great state are still practicing what amounts to slavery. People refuse to let go of the past. Let's get you and the children to a safe place and then we'll see about dealing with these kidnappers."

She dipped her head before she scooted under the wagon. Would this be happening if David was still alive? There had been a few threats before his death but nothing like what had been taking place of late. She pulled a quilt over her and put her hand on her rounded stomach. It didn't matter to her who the father was, but others would not be accepting. She'd have to tell Quinn; he deserved to know who he was defending and the problems that came along with them.

It had been tormenting the night the men had come. Only prayer got her through it and eventually healed her. If she had been a man, they would have just shot her. What did Quinn think? He must have done the math by now and realized this wasn't her husband's child. Starting over would be welcome. If she could find a place where she could hold her head up high, she'd be thrilled. Even if she found such a place, it wouldn't last very long. Sorrow filled her as she turned on her side and fell asleep.

CHAPTER FOUR

Quinn was grateful Heaven could drive the wagon; it gave him time to watch their back. He was fairly certain they were being followed. He needed a plan and he needed it fast. He urged Heaven to drive the horses harder. He spotted a cave, or maybe not. It had been difficult to see from the distance. Now he rode Bandit through trees and brush, and there it was. He hopped down and cautiously explored it. No signs of animals or other people.

Quinn mounted up. "Come on, Bandit. Let's get the others."

It didn't take long to catch up. "Grab what you can and go straight back that way. Take Bandit. There's a cave. I checked it. I'm going to drive the wagon and send it over the side and hopefully it'll break up on its way down the hill."

She opened her mouth, but no words came out, and she quickly closed it and went into action instead. He watched as she filled a quilt with many supplies. She gathered the corners and dragged the bundle as she carried Daisy. Carrying a quilt, Tim followed his mother.

Quinn drove the wagon close to the edge of the drop off,

let the horses go and with enormous effort shoved the wagon off the cliff. It turned over three times before it completely broke apart. With his rifle in one hand, he used heavily leafed branches in his other hand to wipe away his boot prints. Soon he was in the trees. A dust cloud was growing in the distance. The men had found their trail.

Hightailing it, he ran for the cave. Heaven was in there, all ready to shoot. She lay on her stomach with her rifle in her hands. The children were behind her lying on the ground. She knew enough to stay low. He threw his rifle into the cave and dragged big branches dense with foliage to hide the entrance. Then he joined her.

"I sure hope it worked. Were you hurt?" Her voice echoed her worry.

"No, I let the horses go and pushed the wagon over. It flipped a few times. What about Bandit?"

"I grabbed your saddle bags and let him go. He's so well trained, I know he's not too far."

"That's my brother Brogan's handiwork. He's incredible with horses. A few of my other brothers think they're good but they're not as good as Brogan."

She grabbed his biceps, and the jolt that went through him annoyed him. "There they are. Oh my how many are there?"

"About six I believe. There seems to be one who knows what he's doing, and the rest just follow." He shrugged. "Just an observation. They stop then one horse goes and then the others are slow to ride their horses behind him."

She nodded. "They have an Indian guide; they use him to do their dirty work." Pain filled her eyes and she turned her head away.

"Why don't you lay on your side. You can't be comfortable like that. How long do you figure until the baby comes?"

He held his breath. What had he been thinking? He shouldn't have asked such a personal question.

"Two months. I'll need to start sewing diapers soon."

He gazed out at the riders and nodded. He wished he was the type that would throw caution to the wind and tell her she had nothing to worry about, that he'd take care of her. But he wasn't that man. She'd be fine when they got back to the ranch. Maybe one of his eight unmarried brothers would be willing to get hitched or he could set her up with a small house in town.

"They're almost on us." Her voice quavered, and her grip on his arm tightened.

Daisy began to cry and Tim shushed her.

It felt as though all of them in the cave were holding their breath. The men rode by, but that didn't mean they wouldn't circle back.

Heaven's smile was full of hope.

"We wait, they'll be back this way when they don't find us unless they believe we died in the wagon."

"Call me if you need me. I'm going to sit with the children for a while."

"Sure. Tim is a man who can be counted on." He smiled into the darkness. Tim could see him and Quinn hoped to make him feel proud.

The cave was damp, and his leg ached. It made him think of Alicia—or whatever her name was—whenever a part of him hurt. Where was she and what *was* her real name? Why hadn't she said goodbye? He had waited two days not sleeping in his hospital bed, but she'd never returned. No one had been aware of her plan to leave. Finally, someone had been sent around to her residence only to discover that it was empty.

He had fallen into despair and wanted to die. He'd never loved so completely, and she had promised to marry him. He never did find her. Women couldn't be trusted to keep their word. She never meant it when she told him she loved him.

He rubbed his leg and kept watch.

"What's wrong with your leg? Can I help?"

He glanced at Heaven who laid at his side again. "No, I'm better off doing for myself." He didn't miss the frown on her face.

"It looks like they're riding north," she commented.

"If you notice, only four of the six are riding north and their guide isn't with them. We need to be watchful and ready to shoot."

Her eyes widened as she grasped her rifle tighter.

It was a tense hour, and the two lagging riders came close. Heaven had to cover her mouth to stifle a gasp. From the hate in her eyes, Quinn was certain that the Apache had done something to her. The riders stopped and conferred. The Apache pointed back the way they came.

Hopefully, they thought their prey dead. The other man took one more look around and shrugged. They turned their horses and headed back the way from which they had come.

"We'll wait awhile to be sure they aren't coming back, then I'm going to find the horses and we are getting out of here." He handed his canteen to her. "Make sure you and the children drink plenty of water. The trail toward the ranch is a dry dusty ride."

He needed to stand and stretch his leg. There was a vacant cabin not too far from them and it was well hidden. He and Teagan had found it one day long ago.

SHE WASN'T sure he'd find all three horses, but he did. Her heart felt lighter as she watched him approach the cave. She and the children were filthy from head to toe, but it was worth it; they were safe. She smiled at Quinn and got a curt nod in response. He didn't seem much for smiling except at the children.

"I'll put the supplies on one of the wagon horses. You and the children can ride on one and I'll take the other."

"We're ready whenever you are."

He finished dragging the branches away from the cave and tied up the quilt with the belongings on one of the bay horses. Then he lifted Heaven onto the saddled horse. There was something warm in her touch, but he didn't seem to notice. He placed Tim behind her and then Quinn smiled at Daisy as he handed her up in front.

"Thank you."

"Try to keep up with me."

His abruptness confused her. Why was he acting that way? He was kind to Tim and all sweetness to Daisy but brusque with her. Not that it mattered terribly. He was helping them and that was all she needed from him.

The ride took longer than she thought it would. They rode through a forest, and every once in a while, Quinn had her stop so he could backtrack. She thought he had said it would be dry and dusty, but it was cool and a bit damp at times. Maybe he hadn't originally planned to come this way. But she wouldn't say a word. She'd take the shade of a tree over hot and dry any day.

CHAPTER FIVE

*T*he cabin didn't look rundown as she'd expected. It appeared to be a hearty log cabin and that gave her hope that the inside wasn't too bad.

Once again, Quinn was all smiles lifting Tim and Daisy down, but his smile fled when he touched Heaven. Had she done something? Did he just dislike her? Or maybe it was the baby and his mistake of thinking of her a woman without morals. It wouldn't bother her as much if his touch didn't send tingling and fluttering sensations coursing through her. She'd never felt anything like that before.

"Stay out here while I check for animals."

He had his gun drawn and she wasn't so sure it was just animals he was looking for.

"I need to go, Mama," Tim said as he tugged on her skirt. She glanced at the cabin and then led them to a tree they could use. It was big enough to hide behind.

They finished and she led the children back to the cabin and to a scowling Quinn.

"Next time tell me you're going." His voice was tense.

"Of course, I didn't mean to worry you. Did you find anything inside?"

"It's safe to go in. I'll grab the supplies."

Heaven carried Daisy while she held Tim's hand. The inside was nicer than she'd expected. There was a table with four chairs and one bed. Cooking must have been done over the fire, for there was no stove and no place for one. There were a few cobwebs clinging to the ceiling and a lot of dust on all the surfaces, but other than that, it was a fine place.

She put Daisy down and urged Tim to watch her for a minute. The first thing she did was to go to the two windows and test out the shutters. The locks were strong. Then she examined the door. It was thick and heavy. They'd be safe in here for a bit. Her shoulders relaxed for the first time all day. All the traveling and worrying had taken a toll, and weariness overcame her. A thick layer of dust coated the bed, but when she removed the top blanket, the mattress beneath was in decent repair.

"Let's try out the bed." She lifted Daisy in first, then Tim. They scooted over so there was enough room for her and she laid down.

When she woke, she was covered with the quilt they had brought along. The children were playing checkers with Quinn. She smiled, noting that Quinn made sure Daisy got a turn too. She was on his team. That man might act hard-hearted, but he melted when he was with the little ones. He'd find a fine wife someday and have children of his own. A sweet sadness settled on her heart at the thought, but she pushed it aside.

Quinn glanced at her, and his lopsided grin stayed on his face. "We're glad you're up."

"Yes, Quinn said you were being a lazy bones," Tim said very seriously. "Daisy and I wanted to look at your bones, but we weren't allowed."

Her lips twitched. "Quinn is very smart." She would not say about what, but he was smart to let her sleep. She stretched and got out of bed. "I could eat a bear."

"No bear," Daisy said.

"We have rabbits," Tim told her proudly.

"Goodness, how long was I asleep?"

"Long enough so your lazy bones could get rest," Quinn teased. A look of surprise swept over his face. Maybe he wasn't used to smiling or teasing.

There was a fire flickering in the hearth and a pot hanging by a tripod over it. The wonderful smell of rabbit wafted through the cabin.

"How long do you think we'll be here?"

"A couple days at least. The next part of the trip is dry and dusty. The worst part will be that we can be seen for miles on that stretch. If I was watching for us, that's the place I'd watch." He shook his head and glanced around. "There isn't much around here. Maybe you could find someone to take the boys into this cabin. I've never seen anyone here. I'd have to go into town and make sure this parcel of land isn't owned, but that's an easy trip."

She studied their surroundings with a critical eye. "It's a good possibility. I hate thinking of them arriving to my house and finding it empty. May God look over them."

"Yes."

"Mama, I'm hungry. Is the rabbit cooked to a crisp yet?"

"You'll have to ask Quinn and tell him *not* to burn them to a crisp."

Chuckling, Quinn rose as soon as Tim asked him. "Well now, I'd best take a look. Good thinking, partner." He turned the meat one more time. "It'll be ready in a few. I didn't make anything to go with it, except for coffee. Would you like a cup?"

"Please and thank you." She didn't remember her husband

ever pouring her a cup of coffee. It was almost like high society as she accepted the cup from Quinn. She gave him a regal nod. He didn't notice her play, and she supposed that was just as well. He was easy to be around, he didn't have a lot to say. Or so it seemed. At times he looked to be thinking about something serious. His family maybe?

They ate the succulent rabbit, and then she cleaned up. Afterward, she sat in her chair and smiled at her young ones. Tim looked so much like his father and Daisy favored her. She touched her burgeoning belly, and she already knew the baby would favor its father. She refused to think just how hard it would be to raise such a child.

"Tell you what, if you two can be in bed quickly, I'll tell you a story about me and my brothers."

"Oh yes!" Tim looked through the clothes but only found a shirt. "What am I to do now?"

"I'll take you out to the outhouse now and then you can sleep in the shirt and your underclothes tonight."

Tim's eyes lit up. "Is that fine with you Mama?"

She smiled and nodded. "I'll change Daisy and see what other clothes I grabbed." She waited until they left before she searched to see if there was anything for her to wear. There was nothing. She'd sleep in her dress again. Maybe that was just as well. If she'd had anything she would have wanted to be changed before Quinn and Tim came back. They probably wouldn't take long.

Daisy was propped up on the bed and her cheeks were pink while her eyes brightened when Quinn walked in. Timmy ran and somehow took his trousers off at the same time. Heaven shook her head. She watched as Tim jumped into the bed and made room for Quinn to sit on the bed with them. Quinn turned toward her for permission. She nodded.

She got his bedroll ready for him in front of the hearth.

She made sure the window shutters were locked as well as the door. When she sat, she felt the pressure that told her she should have made a trip to the privy herself.

Quinn stopped his storytelling as soon as Daisy and Tim closed their eyes. He walked toward her. "Is something wrong?"

"Yes, I should have used the outhouse earlier and now the baby is pushing against me."

Quinn nodded and lit a lantern. "Come, I'll walk you."

"But the children—"

"Will be just fine." He grabbed a rifle before they left and walked before her, lighting the path.

"I'm so sorry to put you out."

"Nonsense."

Her face heated as she went in. He was a stranger and he knew what she was doing. She got a hold of herself. Everyone knew what people did in the outhouse. She was no shy miss anymore.

When she was done, she walked out with her head high. She stopped at the pump and washed her hands. "Thank you," she whispered. "I would have changed while you were out with Tim, but I didn't manage to bring anything else to wear, so I'll have to wear my dress." She opened the door and Quinn ushered her in first.

He went to his saddle bag and grabbed out a fresh shirt. "You take this and be comfortable. I'll keep my back to you, don't worry."

She took the blue shirt and nodded. He had a caring way about him, and he was a gentleman too. How he still had a fresh shirt after traveling by horse surprised her. His shirt when she had first seen him had looked to be on the clean side too.

She settled the shirt over her body and sighed. He was

right, it was much more comfortable than her dress, which was stretched to the limit. The shirt fell below her knees, almost to her ankles. He was much bigger than her husband had been. She was grateful.

CHAPTER SIX

*H*eaven stared into the flames that danced gently across the logs in the fireplace. She should get up and stoke them to keep the blaze going, but she was worn out. Her arms and legs felt as though weighed down by stones. She took a deep breath and slowly released it, giving in to the lethargy.

They'd been in the cabin for three days. In the morning, they planned to leave. Heaven didn't know why but her energy had depleted rapidly and she had slept the greater part of each day. Would she be able to ride a horse? She didn't have a choice, but it was going to be uncomfortable. Her back hurt like never before. Quinn said they'd camp out one, maybe two nights before they would be on his property. He really hadn't been very far from home. He'd said he had left his home and had just ridden around looking for a place to fit in. She wasn't sure what he meant by that, and he hadn't told her why he had found such a thing necessary.

What if he decided that he still didn't fit with his family and left her there? It wasn't as though she was his responsibility, and he'd gone far beyond what any other man would have.

"Can I get you anything?"

She smiled up at him. "No, you've been wonderful to me, to us all. We've never been treated so gently. I've never known a man who could be so attentive. I come from a long line of people where the man was king and the woman his servant." She swallowed hard. "Is there something I can do for *you*? Without you, we'd be dead."

He stared at her with a blank expression on his face. Then he reached over and put his hand over hers. "I don't want to ever hear you offering something to me or any man. You are better than that. Has anyone ever taken—" He stared at her stomach.

"Oh my, no! I—this child — No, I wasn't doing any favor when this baby was made. I bled so and I could hardly walk for a week." Her chest tightened as the memories swamped her, and she drew a deep breath before she went on. "My eye was swollen shut, and I couldn't open my mouth wide enough to eat. I never knew pain could be so bad. It's a wonder I survived. I don't think they intended me to." Chills raced up and down her spine. "I'd had my children hide where I usually hid the Negro boys. If I hadn't—they would have taken my babies and sold them. I could hardly move afterwards, but I could sit by the window with my rifle loaded." She hung her head. She couldn't bear the pity in Quinn's eyes, and suddenly she wished she'd never told him. Shame filled her and her eyes filled. Hastily she wiped the tears away.

He didn't move, didn't speak.

"I shouldn't have told you," she decided aloud. "I didn't mean to place my burdens on you. I'd best get some sleep." She shook her head. "What you must think of me..." No sooner had she stood, when the next thing she knew she was drawn on to Quinn's lap. He pulled her close and placed her head on his shoulder. At first, she stiffened but fairly quickly, she was holding on to him just as tight. She wept as she never had, and it was pure anguish remembering it all, but it was also cleansing. She finally leaned back and took his face in her hands and she kissed his cheek.

"Thank you," she whispered before she stood again and went to bed. She fell asleep immediately.

HE LAY in front of the fire unable to sleep. What had he just done? Had she read anything into his comfort? He hoped not. What if she started looking at him in some special way? He was just helping her and her family and that was it. There were no emotional strings. He could easily drop her off at Teagan's ranch and leave again.

That still stuck in his craw; Teagan was the only brother listed on the property. It was a betrayal of how they'd all lived their lives as brothers. He was just as good if not better at ranching than his brother. This was his father's fault; he'd made the will. What had he'd been thinking? Was there one of them his father didn't trust? Was it because of Brogan, the son he'd fathered with the neighbor's wife? Had the hatred between the families caused his father to become nervous? Maybe he was afraid his ranch would somehow become Maguire land. Whatever the reason it hurt him to his soul. Teagan, his brother, his best friend, had known the whole time and never said a word. He'd allowed all the brothers to assume they all had equal shares.

Turning over, he saw Heaven gazing at him. Was she thinking about wedding bells? Disturbed by the disastrous thought, he threw the covers off and put on his gun belt and coat.

"Where are you going?" She sounded worried.

"I just need some air. Go to sleep." He shoved his hat on his head and quietly opened the door, stepped out, and closed it behind him. He kicked around a bit until he found a piece of wood that looked interesting. He turned it over and over, studying it. Then he pulled out his hunting knife, sat on a tree stump, and began to whittle. What he wanted and what was happening were two different things. He wanted to be alone. He craved solitude, didn't he?

Pieces of the branch he was carving on flew, dropping to the ground around him in chunks and curls. He scraped the knife along one of the rough edges and just barely avoided taking a piece out of his thumb.

Fury surged as he stared at the knife and the wood that had been nearly whittled to nothing. Angry with himself for getting into such a sticky predicament, he hurled the wood across the clearing. It had been his own fault. He'd still been wandering because he'd held on to Teagan's betrayal to keep himself from going home. But the way their father's will had been written wasn't something Teagan could have controlled. He should have told them, but it hadn't been such a grievous wrong, certainly nothing worth getting so mad about.

Quinn sighed. It also wasn't Heaven's fault that he was helping her. He'd just ridden into that one; it wasn't like she had asked him to intervene. But now... Now he was angry because he'd enjoyed having her in his arms. He knew how it would all end, and there were children involved this time. Children he already cared about. He needed to get his heart hardened against all women again. Heaven had made a small crack and it needed fixing.

He sat again, staring into the woods, and let the memories come upon him. They were never far away.

Everywhere he went, he had smelled the hospital. The cleaning scent, the medical scent, the odor of blood and the wretched stench of death. No matter how hard he scrubbed, no matter how long it had been, he carried the stink on him. He groaned as he flexed the muscles across his back. His flesh had healed finally, but his back and part of his chest were covered in scars, and the skin grew tight at times.

He'd thought he looked hideous, but Alicia had made him feel like a normal man. She often sat with him during her breaks and then one day they started talking about a future together. She wove such a lovely picture, and he fell for it as hard as he'd fallen for her.

An owl hooted from deep in the woods. He ran his hand over his face. Remembering was working; his heart was in unbearable pain. Heaven wouldn't be able to get in. Not after how he had suffered at Alicia's coldhearted hands. He stood and went inside. He didn't feel as troubled. He'd be able to sleep.

The next morning, he tried his best to stay out of Heaven's way. When he did gaze at her, the bewilderment and hurt on her face made him feel guilty. He made no promises, so why should she should act hurt? Even little Tim gave him a glare.

"Ready? I want to get as far as we can."

Heaven nodded. "Everything is packed, and the children are ready." She led Tim and Daisy out of the cabin without glancing at him.

He grabbed the supplies and loaded up the horse. He then helped Heaven onto the saddle and lifted Tim, so he sat behind her. "I'll take Daisy for a while and give you a rest." He saw the beginning of a nod before he bent and took the girl into his arms.

Daisy smiled at him and patted his face. All his irritation melted away. She sure made the world light up just like — No, he refused to think about it.

He placed her in front of him and she said, "Giddy up!"

It might have been nice to share an amused smile with Heaven. His chest tightened, and his heart seemed to twinge with longing. This was going to be much harder that he had thought. They rode for a while, and he glanced at Heaven. Her face was pale, and she seemed in pain.

Concern for her welfare led to guilt for how hard he was driving her and the children.

"Are you all right?"

"I'm perfectly fine."

She was a stubborn one.

"We're taking a break." He just wished he had more than a few rocks for shade. He lowered himself down with Daisy in his arm. He set her down and then turned to get Tim. Quinn received another glare from the boy. He set him on the ground. "Look after Daisy for a minute."

He met Heaven's gaze as he held his arms up for her. His heart ached at the hurt and shadows in her eyes. Carefully, he helped her down, but he didn't let go.

"What's going on? I can see you're in pain."

She quickly stepped away from him. "It's nothing, but a rest will be welcome."

He took her hand and led her to one of the bigger rocks, kicking some loose gravel out of the way before he sat her down so she could lean against it. He then made sure everyone had plenty of water. He watched the flat land around him for any other riders. He didn't see a thing, in particular not any kind of dust cloud to indicate riders. But he also watched Heaven, and she winced when she moved. Were her legs sore from riding? She likely hadn't ridden much if she had no call to do so. He needed to get them to the ranch. But would she be able to ride eight more hours? He doubted it. Regret for the sacrifice of the wagon plagued him, though there had seemed little choice at the time.

They rested for about a half hour before he got ready to go again. He checked over the horses, then turned back to the group. The children were on their feet, but their mother wasn't.

Quinn squatted next to her. "Need some help?"

Lines of pain and exhaustion were etched into her face, and her eyes swam with tears. "I don't want to be a bother," she said, her voice barely above a whisper.

"Didn't that husband of yours ever tell you that you could never be a bother?" He grinned at her, but his grin faded as she shook her head. He helped her to her feet, and she stumbled when she took her first step. He swept her up into his arms. "I wish I had a way to make it easier."

She touched his cheek. "I'll be fine. I can grit my teeth with the best of them." She winced as soon as she was on the horse, but she swung her leg over and held her arms out for Daisy.

Daisy shook her head. "No, Mama."

"What do you mean, 'no, Mama'?" Quinn asked.

"I lub you." She smiled sweetly at him, and his heart thawed.

"That's very sweet and all, but your Mama…"

"No!" Daisy seemed to be the most stubborn female he ever did meet.

"It's fine. Tim come ride with me. I'd rather not force Daisy. I'm not up for it."

Daisy smiled again. She leaned in and kissed him three times on his cheek. "I lub you and Tim and Mama. I think I lub you mostest." She seemed very proud of herself.

He couldn't help but smile, and this time he included Heaven and Tim in his smile. "Let's ride to safety. I was going to ride around the town, but we'll ride through it. It'll be safer and a bit faster. I'm hoping that you'll have a bed to sleep on soon." He gazed at Heaven while he talked, but it was Daisy who said, "Thank you."

"Take care of your ma," he told Tim.

"Yes, sir."

He mounted the horse with Daisy in his arms and took a last look around. Something had changed about the horizon. *Dang!* Someone was stirring up the dirt. Even if they were riding hard, though, they were hours away, and there was a good chance they hadn't been spotted by whoever was coming in their direction.

"Go slow," he told Heaven. "I don't want to kick up too much dust."

Her mouth formed an O, then it flattened into a grim line and she nodded.

Off they went riding, nice and slow. An uneasiness settled over Quinn and refused to go away. They needed to go south and get back into the trees. It would take longer, but hopefully he'd be able to keep everyone safe. They would have to ride as long as the sun was up, and even then, he planned to lead the horses himself. Would Heaven be able to make it? He could make a travois for her and if she held Daisy it should work out. But that would be cumbersome and could slow them if they needed to make a run for it.

They rode for two hours before they came to the woods. Heaven's face was a mask of pain. He called a halt, and he and Daisy got down. He took Tim off the horse first. "Watch Daisy for a minute, Tim. I need to have a word with your mother."

Tim nodded.

Quinn gazed up at Heaven. "I'm going to lie out my

bedroll and put you on it to rest a bit while I make a travois for you and Daisy."

The relief on her face was great. She groaned when he lifted her off the horse and laid her down.

"You rest."

CHAPTER SEVEN

*I*t would be so easy to let Quinn take care of her forever, but that wasn't how life worked. No, he might be helping for now, but in the end, she and the children would be on their own. She gritted her teeth. Her back hurt something awful.

Please Lord, don't let anything be wrong with the baby. Please keep us all safe.

Right away, Quinn set about crafting the travois. He looked as though he knew what he was doing. It couldn't have been over twenty minutes when he told her he was done. He packed everything up and attached the travois to the bay. He laid his blanket down first and then doubled one of the quilts. He was so very gentle when he helped her to her feet.

The next thing she knew, he'd swung her up in his strong arms and placed her on the travois. He went back and lifted Daisy, who'd fallen asleep, and put the child tight against her.

"Hold your arm around her," he instructed, and then he took the last quilt and bundled them into it.

When he picked up the length of rope, her eyes widened.

"What's that for?" All the possibilities suggested by the rope struck fear into her chest.

"I need to strap you in. It's rocky and I don't want you or Daisy flying through the air and hitting a tree."

"Hitting a tree? That really happens?" She cocked her right brow.

He gave an exaggerated shrug and smiled. "I'm sure it has to someone somewhere. Just humor me."

She laughed until the rope went around their bodies. It was creepy, like they were going to be buried or something. It was hard, but she didn't glare at him. He left one arm free and handed her the end of the rope. Maybe it would be fine after all.

"We need to travel a long while. If you need anything just yell out and I'll stop. We should be in town a little after sunset."

She nodded. "Thank you, Quinn."

His face grew red, and he hurried away. She'd embarrassed him and that hadn't been her intent. The creaking of leather told her he was mounting. Then Tim and Quinn were ready to go. She and Daisy were last in line. There was a sudden jolt and they were on their way. It was bumpy and at times she winced, but she wouldn't have been able to ride any further.

Daisy woke and after she got over her initial fear, she thought it a fun adventure. She laughed and giggled whenever they hit a bump. It did Heaven's spirit good.

Quinn had been right about it being a long ride. He led the horses when it became dark and she worried about Tim being on a horse alone.

"I can see the town lights!" Quinn called back to her.

"Thank goodness." She was exhausted and hurting.

It took longer than she'd imagined, but soon they were on a road with buildings on each side of them. Most were shut for the night, but it was a relief to have help in case the men following them rode in. They stopped in front of a hotel, and her breath caught. She'd never stayed in a hotel before.

He glanced at her and smiled, but the concern in his eyes was evident. He lifted Daisy and set her on her feet. "Tim, take her to the outside of that door right there," Quinn said, pointing to the hotel door. "But don't go inside."

He then swung her up as easily as if she weighed nothing at all. "Is the baby all right?"

"I think so."

"I'll get you settled and then send for the doctor."

She gave him a watery smile. "I don't know if I'll ever be able to pay you back."

"We're friends. We don't keep a tally."

As he and Heaven approached the door, Tim held the door open for them all. As soon as they entered a hulking giant of a man with a large engaging smile bounded toward them.

"Congratulations, Quinn! You've finally gone and done it! You must have kept it under wraps I hadn't heard a word of you marrying. Picked a right pretty gal too. Let me get you all a room."

"Who is that?" she whispered.

"Glen Pickford, the owner, and the man behind the counter is Luke Wilton."

"Oh…" The heat that had flooded her face upon the man's greeting increased. It was obvious Quinn was known here, and his friends had made a very wrong assumption. He hadn't corrected Mr. Pickford, so she didn't know if she should say anything or not.

"I think—" Quinn started.

"I have the perfect room for you and your family, Mr. Kavanagh," Luke told them as he approached, a broad smile lighting his face. "Follow me."

She waited for Quinn to say something, but yet again he didn't. He'd set them straight later, she supposed.

Luke opened the door and stepped to the side, revealing two big beds inside. Quinn set her down.

"I need Dr. Bright to come now."

Luke nodded. "I'll send for him right away and then make sure food and the like is brought to your room." He closed the door on his way out.

"Quinn, we're not married." Heaven clutched his arm and tugged urgently. Her name would be pulled through the mud again.

"I know, I'll get everything right as soon as the doctor comes."

She nodded, but she knew that by then it wouldn't make a bit of difference. Food was sent and the children ate. She was too exhausted to even notice what it was, but they seemed content enough and ate their fill. Heaven watched Quinn take off their shoes and tuck them into the other bed. They were asleep before their heads hit their pillows.

Her eyes were drifting closed but then there was a knock on the door. Quinn opened it a little and peered out, then opened it the rest of the way and welcomed the man on the other side.

The doctor was young and very handsome. So much so, that he was probably already married. He asked her a few personal questions. After the first question Quinn walked to the other side of the room and looked out the window, making it obvious that he was not listening.

"Quinn," Dr. Bright called, "are you taking her to the ranch?"

He turned. "That was the plan."

"She'll need at least two weeks of bedrest, or the baby is bound to make an appearance early. Just tell Dolly, she'll know what to do. Congratulations on your new family!"

And as quick as that, Dr. Bright left.

She had to say something to him, they had to discuss her situation.

"Quinn," she whispered. A lone tear trailed down her cheek. "People think we're married, and they darn sure know we are in this room together. You need to set them straight. I won't be able to get away from this area with the baby, and I'm so tired of people turning their backs on me. Decent people won't talk to me. Believe me, Quinn, I know how it feels and I don't want that for me or my children. As soon as people see the baby, they'll shun me."

The bed dipped as he sat on it. "I'll make things right. Now why would anyone shun you?"

"The man who meted out my punishment was the Indian. The others cheered him on. He's—he's the baby's father." She closed her eyes. Quinn was bound to be scowling at her. She heard his boots drop. Then he lay next to her on his side facing her. She opened her eyes and turned her head toward him.

Kindness shone in his eyes. "I'm so sorry for what you've been through. It's not right, and it's not fair." He gazed deep into her eyes. Was he trying to see inside her or trying to tell her something without saying the words? "The men wanted you shamed for life. It's not the baby's fault."

She shook her head. "I'd never take my anger out on the babe."

He put his hand gently over her belly. "You need to get some rest."

Her body began to shake. She was scared, so scared. How was she going to support her children? No one would hire her, and even if they did, she couldn't leave the children alone so she could work. And if the baby came too soon, it might not survive. She rolled onto her side with her back toward him, though that didn't help. She could still sense his nearness.

Then he shifted closer and he was embracing her from the back.

"What are you doing?" she hissed.

"Spooning you," he murmured. His breath was warm against the back of her neck. "Didn't your husband ever hold you or comfort you this way?"

"No." Then, realizing that sounded harsh, she quickly added, "He was a good man, though, and he provided for us."

Quinn wrapped his arms the rest of the way around her. "Try to relax, everything will be fine. Tomorrow we'll go to the ranch, and our housekeeper, Dolly and Teagan's wife Gemma will take care of you. I won't let anyone hurt you."

The shaking slowed and then stopped, and she was able to relax. Quinn didn't understand, she'd already *been* hurt. But going to his ranch sounded wonderful. She'd do her share of the work. No one would have to take care of her. A sigh slipped out. It felt so nice, so warm, so safe being in Quinn's arms. Her husband had hardly ever touched her. Had he ever hugged her? She couldn't think of an instance when he had.

Quinn would have to make sure everyone knew they weren't married and nothing had happened between them. He had to. She fell asleep wondering if his brothers were nice.

There was a knock on the door the next morning. It was loud and insistent. Quinn eased off the bed and answered the door. His brother Sullivan pushed his way in. His eyes grew wide and then he turned and gave Quinn an angry stare.

"I don't see no wedding ring, brother. I couldn't believe

what I was hearing over at the general store. Did I miss your wedding? The Quinn I know would never compromise a woman. In fact, the Quinn I know *hates* women."

Quinn turned when he heard Heaven getting up. "Get back to bed. This is just my brother, Sullivan. He likes to spout off for no reason."

"No reason?" Sullivan sputtered, staring with wide eyes at Heaven. "She's pregnant? Quinn, why didn't you tell us you have a woman friend?"

"Time to go, Sullivan."

"How are you planning to get your family to the ranch?" His brother planted his feet wide and gave a challenging glare. "I heard tell you all came in on horseback pulling your woman on a travois. I have the wagon. You might as well come with me. I'll pretend I knew you were married. Now, why is—? Beg pardon, ma'am, I don't know your name."

"I'm Heaven, and this is Tim and Daisy."

Tim looked uncertain while Daisy gave Sullivan a sparkling smile. Daisy got out of bed and ran to Quinn with her arms raised. He immediately scooped her up.

"I lub you," she said and then she kissed Quinn's cheek.

The surprise on Sullivan's face was priceless. "What? You don't think me lovable?" Quinn asked seriously

Sullivan chuckled. "My opinion doesn't matter, Daisy's does. I'm going back to the store and getting something soft for Heaven to lie on. And I'll add a little gossip of my own. I'll be back and then we can go."

After Sullivan left, Quinn sat on the bed next to Heaven with Daisy in his arms.

"I'm so sorry. I've caused you too much trouble." Heaven's eyes teared.

"Don't worry about it. We'll get you out to the ranch. That's all that matters. I will leave and you can get dressed.

I'll be in the lobby." He slung the saddle bags over his shoulder and left.

Quinn nodded politely at the few people who passed through the lobby while he waited. He went outside when Sullivan stopped the wagon in front of the hotel.

"You'd better announce you're married, or Heaven will be tarred and feathered. Did you know you're considered quite the catch? Many ladies had their eye on you. Unhappy women are gathering in the general store." Sullivan's brow furrowed. "I don't remember you having any lady friends."

"I didn't. Listen, Heaven and I—"

"Save it." He reached into his pocket and took out a wedding ring. "I told them your story of how you rescued the family and you fell in love. You married her but didn't have a ring, and you thought to wait until after the baby to get one since her fingers are swollen."

Quinn drew his brows together as he studied his brother. "When did you become such a story teller?"

"The ladies all ate it up and told me to get a cheap one now and a better one after she has the baby. You are such a romantic hero marrying a woman pregnant by her late husband. I almost teared up."

"You are such a bad egg!" He spotted Heaven and Tim and Daisy making their way across the lobby. Hurrying over, he lifted the bag from Heaven's grasp. "You could have waited, and I could have gotten the bag." He glanced up and saw a flock of people coming their way. He took the ring and put it on Heaven's ring finger. "Just go with it. Apparently, I broke a few hearts by marrying you."

Her eyes went wide, and then she laughed. "Whatever it takes to make you look good. I'd hate for your name to be muddied by me." Her smile faded and she stared down at the ground.

"If we hurry there won't be much conversation."

Quinn and Sullivan made short work of laying out the blankets. As the crowd drew closer, Quinn picked her up and gently put her in the wagon and then lifted Tim and Daisy into the back.

"What about the horses?" Heaven asked.

"I'll have one of the men come and get them."

Sullivan yelled, "Yaw!" and they made record time leaving town. A little ways out, though, he stopped the wagon. "We need to make sure the quilts are making your wife comfortable."

Quinn glanced over his shoulder. Heaven's face was very pale. Quickly he turned and climbed over the seat to the back of the wagon. Everything was askew, and Heaven wasn't even on the quilts.

"I'm sorry. You must be in pain."

"I was just thinking how as we should have tied me up like you did yesterday." She tried to laugh, but it came out more like a wheeze.

Behind him, Sullivan chuckled, and Quinn figured he'd have to explain her remark at some point. He piled the quilts and made a sort of nest for her and the children. The smile she gave him made him feel unworthy. How was he going to explain to everyone they weren't married? Dolly would have his hide and Teagan...

"Are we set?" he asked.

Daisy had tears flowing down her face. He moved close to the little girl. "Daisy, what is it?"

"You didn't ask me to sit on your lap. You don't lub me."

"Daisy," Heaven whispered.

"I got it. Daisy would you do me the honor of sitting on my lap?" He almost went flying over the side of the wagon as Daisy stood and launched herself at him. Heaven's face had a rosy color to it now.

With everyone comfortable enough, they continued on at

51

a more reasonable pace. Daisy babbled at him and kept kissing his cheek. Sullivan wore an amused expression, and Quinn wondered how he would explain everything to the others.

Somehow, though, the cat was out of the bag. Most of the people on the ranch were gathered around smiling and happy as they drove up. Some folks kept secrets forever, but not in this family it seemed. He smiled and held on to Daisy.

"My word, Quinn, you have yourself a nice-looking family!" Dolly held her arms up to Daisy who held on to Quinn too tightly around his neck. "Gracious, you don't want to meet me?"

Daisy shook her head. "I lub my dada."

Flames licked at his skin as the heat of embarrassment crept up his neck and flooded his face.

Tim stood. "Hi!" he said. He stared at Dolly. "Do you make cookies? You can help me down." Tim had made a conquest, it seemed, and Quinn couldn't wait to see how long it took for Dolly to make the first batch of cookies.

He set Daisy down and then climbed into the wagon and leaned close to Heaven. "Are you all right?" he whispered.

"There are many people here."

"Yes, there are. Just let them believe what they believe until I can straighten it out." He lifted her as she nodded, and then he started to put her down on the back end of the wagon so he could jump down and pick her up.

"Here, hand her to me," Teagan said. "I've been hoping each day you'd be back."

Quinn handed Heaven to him. "Heaven, this is my brother, Teagan."

"Oh, I've heard of you. Quinn speaks of you often."

Teagan cocked his brow and smiled. He glanced at Quinn as he hopped from the wagon.

"I can take her."

"Of course." Teagan put her into Quinn's arms.

She giggled. "I feel like I'm being passed around."

"I have seven more brothers you have yet to meet, remember?" He chuckled as he kept an eye on the children. Dolly was herding them toward the house.

Gemma, Teagan's wife opened the door. "I would have come out, but I was fixing up the couch so you can rest."

"I'm Heaven."

"It's so very nice to meet you, I'm Gemma. Thank you for bringing Quinn home. He's been missed." Gemma smiled at him.

It was noisy, and Quinn worried about Heaven getting enough rest, but before long all his brothers left except for Teagan and Sullivan.

Gemma gazed from one brother to another. "What's happened?"

CHAPTER EIGHT

*H*eaven's nerves were stretched to the limit. Dolly took Daisy and Tim into the kitchen. Quinn sat down as though he didn't have many things to explain. What would they say when they discovered the truth?

"When are you due?" Gemma asked. "Your other two children are beautiful."

"The doctor told me less than six weeks. I thought I had two more months. I'm to stay in bed for a day or two."

"Weeks," Quinn corrected her. "You are to stay in bed for weeks."

His stubborn eyes widened when he met her stubborn gaze.

Quinn released an exasperated sigh. "Fine. We'll take it day by day," he conceded.

"I think you'll make a fine husband and father," Gemma said. "Congratulations,"

Heaven waited for Quinn to say something, but he remained silent. Sullivan didn't act as though anything was wrong.

Oh bother, it'll just make leaving that much harder. So, she'd stay until the baby could travel, and then she'd go; where, she didn't know, but she was strong and capable. She would not be the one to tell the truth; it wasn't her family.

"Why don't Sullivan and I take the children outside so you can rest, Heaven?"

Tim ran into the room. "Can we, Ma?"

She nodded. "Of course."

Daisy went to Quinn and lifted her arms. "I lub you."

This time Quinn kissed her cheek. "I love you too."

A brighter smile never was. And her pure, innocent smile caused everyone else to smile too.

"You go with Teagan and Sullivan," Quinn told her. "They're my brothers, and they're fun to play with."

Daisy wiggled her way down and stood in front of Teagan. She hit him in the leg. "You're it!" she yelled as she ran out the house.

"If you'd rather, I can show you to Quinn's room. It might be more restful," Gemma offered. She seemed like a nice woman.

"Well, Quinn and I—"

"That's a good idea, Gemma," Quinn interrupted. "Has Brogan come home?"

Gemma shook her head.

"He's over at the Maguire Ranch. Living there he is. Gemma has been very generous to him," Dolly told him.

"The kids can have his room then," Quinn decided out loud.

"You know the foreman's house is sitting empty…" Dolly suggested.

Quinn gazed at Heaven. "We can talk about it later. I'd like to take her upstairs."

Heaven sat up and put her feet on the floor but she didn't have time to stand before she was snatched up into Quinn's arms. She let out a little squeal. She stayed quiet until they were in his very large room with a very large bed. He sat her on the bed and put pillows behind her back.

"Well?" She tried to scowl, but she ended up smiling.

Quinn leaned against the closed door with his arms crossed. "Well what?"

She sighed and looked up at the ceiling. She shook her head and then leveled a stare at him. "You didn't tell anyone we're not married. You said you'd take care of it."

"I didn't want you embarrassed, and I kept thinking about the baby. You, the children, and the baby all need protection, and marrying me would do just that. I'm not saying it's a love match, but I can't in good conscience tell anyone the truth just now. It might put you and your little ones in harm's way."

Heaven clasped her hands together and stared down at them. What was he saying exactly? Was this farce to go on or was he asking her to marry him?

"You don't love me." She gave him a sad smile.

"Plenty of people get married for reasons other than love. I have no love to give a woman. That part of my heart was broken off, and it never mended. I do admire you. You're a woman of wisdom and strength. You are courageous, and if I had a best friend, I'd want that friend to be you." He pushed off the door and strode to the bed and then sat next to her. "No one need ever know, and as soon as I can make private arrangements, I will legally marry you." He put his hand over her clasped ones.

"It feels strange wearing a wedding band." She stared down at the simple ring. "I've never had one before." After a moment, she drew a fortifying breath and released it. "Very well, I seem to have no other choice unless I want to be branded a liar. How did we get into this situation? I never planned to marry again. I knew no one would want me with an Indian child." She sat up, determined to show strength.

"But this will not be a child of my shaming, it will be a child of my courage. How I survived, I don't know." She smiled as hope blossomed within her heart. "Quinn Kavanagh, I accept your proposal, and it's no hardship to pretend to be your bride. You've become a friend like no other. You are so different from David. He was a good man, but he didn't appreciate my opinion. He never hit me, though oftentimes when he was displeased, he gave me a look." She shrugged. "But I had a roof over my head and two precious children and believe it or not it was his decision to make our home a safe place for the Negro children. Yes, Quinn, I will accept the protection you can give us."

He leaned closer, and she got ready to be kissed, but at the last minute, he pulled away and stood. "I'll come get you for supper and don't worry about the little ones." He stepped through the door and closed it behind him.

It was too much too fast. She wasn't still grieving for a husband who never hugged her. She had come to terms with that a while ago. A pretend marriage and then a real ceremony. Would it ever happen that way? Quinn could ask her to leave whenever he wanted. He wasn't like that, but it was a possibility. And what would she say to his family? That she had promised to pretend they were married until they actually were? Who would believe that? She sighed. Daisy was already so attached to him. He was a kind, affectionate man who listened, but she never wanted another man who could tell her what to do all day. So it was a risk but one she'd need to take. She closed her eyes.

"We need to whisper," Quinn said to Daisy, who was in his arms looking at her mother.

"Am I whisperin'?"

His lips twitched as she practically yelled. "That's loud."

"Now?" She gazed into his eyes looking for confirmation.

"Tell you what, tidbit, why don't I put you on the bed and you can give your mama a kiss? Kisses are good to wake up to." He saw Heaven trying her hardest not to smile as he set Daisy down next to her mama's head.

Daisy stared at Heaven's face. Then she leaned over and pried one eyelid open. She did the same to the other. "Are you awake?" Daisy planted kisses all over Heaven's face.

Heaven laughed. "I'm awake!" She hugged Daisy to her and glowed, her joy unmistakable. Then she turned her gaze to him and gave him a look that clearly said wait until your turn.

"Do you want me to carry you to the table or would you like to eat up here?"

"I'd like to meet your family. Can you hand me my hairbrush?"

He found it and handed it to her. All the pins were out of her hair and waves of blond tresses fell almost to her waist. The glorious golden mass made his fingers itch to see if it was as silky as it looked. Quickly, he turned away. He couldn't give into temptation; it wasn't right.

He gazed out the window, but he was listening to Heaven and Daisy chatter. It seemed Daisy was insisting on helping. Heaven could threaten to shoot a man down and she also was a gentle mother. He turned and smiled. "Don't you both look so beautiful?"

"Was that a question, Quinn?"

His face heated. "No of course not. Now let me get my two favorite pretty ladies to the table. Daisy, I'll carry you first. Make sure to smile at all my brothers; they love smiles."

He carried her to the table, and Tim scowled. "What happened to her hair?"

Quinn gave Tim a serious look. "Having one braid up on your head and the other hanging down is the fashion."

He set Daisy down on a chair. "Watch her while I get her mother." When he glanced over his shoulder, he saw Daisy bestowing each of his brothers with a wide, sunny smile.

Heaven looked more rested than he'd ever seen her. Her hair was sticking up in various places, but he didn't mention it. "Ready?"

She nodded. "It's very strange to meet people who don't have a clue about my recent past."

"You have nothing to be ashamed of." He scooped her up. "You need to eat more; you were heavier the first time I lifted you."

Her face turned crimson. "Mr. Kavanagh, a man never mentions a lady's weight."

"Frankly, I have no idea about things like that. I don't speak to many women. But the truth is the truth. We have a baby to think of."

Her eyes flickered, and a knot formed in his stomach. When had he started thinking about the baby being theirs? Heaven had the ability to hurt him deeply, and he couldn't... he just couldn't.

He placed Heaven on a chair. "Heaven, this is Donnell, Murphy, Fitzpatrick, Angus, Rafferty and Shea. You already met Teagan and Sullivan." He gestured to each as he introduced them. Then Tim raised his hand. "And you know Tim and Daisy, I believe," he added with a smile.

He smiled as Gemma and Dolly joined them.

"It's nice to meet you. Quinn talks about you all."

Fitzpatrick laughed. "Quinn talks?"

"I swear he goes days without uttering a word," Donnell teased.

Heaven put her hand over his, and warmth bloomed in his face. "Quinn is a very good conversationalist. He's not the type that goes on and on about nothing. I enjoy talking with him." She squeezed his hand and he wanted nothing more than to pull away from her grasp. She was getting under his skin.

"Quinn, why is your face red? Do you have a fever?" Tim asked as he stared. "My face gets real red when I have a fever."

Daisy stood up on the chair. "My dada is good. I lub him. I like red." She put her hands on her little hips and gave Donnell and Fitzpatrick glares.

Quinn thought his heart would burst. He quickly stood and picked Daisy up off the chair before she fell. He sat with her on his lap. He'd have to make this all work, at the very least for Daisy's sake. She tilted her head all the way back and smiled.

He quickly glanced at Heaven, noting the tears streaming down her face. His stomach clenched. This time he put his hand over hers. But this had to be the last time he'd touch her; it was so dangerous.

"Quinn is my daddy too." Tim gazed at Quinn with an almost pleading expression.

"Of course I'm your daddy, Tim. We're a family, and now you have too many uncles to count. They are my brothers. Gemma is my sister and she's married to Teagan, and Dolly is like a mother to us all, a very young mother," he amended quickly.

Tim jumped down and buried his face in Quinn's side then wrapped his arms as far as they would go around.

Quinn wasn't sure he'd be able to get through supper without a tear of his own appearing. He heard a few sniffles. Apparently his brothers felt the same.

"That's right, I'm young and in charge." Dolly smiled. "I have apple pie for dessert for those who eat their supper."

Gemma and Teagan exchanged a look. Gemma had once

decided to marry a widower and most of the brothers had eaten one slice out of each pie that she had baked to bring to a barn raising to meet those men. They'd thought she'd stay home, but it didn't stop her.

Tim ran back to his seat and dug in. Daisy helped herself from Quinn's plate.

"Daisy—"

"Heaven, it's fine. We have plenty of time to teach manners."

"I know I'm still learning," Fitzpatrick said with a chuckle.

For a moment, Quinn wanted to leave. He wanted to get on Bandit and disappear to a place where there weren't feelings or children or a woman so sweet. His heart pounded, and he couldn't breathe. What was he supposed to do with a family?

"Quinn, let's go outside and grab some air. You look pale," Teagan suggested.

The perfect escape. Teagan knew him too well. Nodding, he stood reseated the children and then followed his oldest brother out the front door. They walked to one of their cattle pastures and stood watched them for a time.

"We sure have a lot of cattle," Quinn said, unable to count them all or even guess how many head were grazing just in this pasture.

"Yes, we do. Want to talk about what's eating at you?"

Quinn took a deep breath. "I don't have any love to give, Teagan. I got nothing left, and eventually Heaven will wilt from the lack of it. Daisy keeps telling me she loves me, and Tim called me his daddy. None of it is real, and people are going to get hurt." He swallowed and kept his gaze fixed on the pasture. Might as well tell it all. "Truth is, I walked into a gunfight and walked out with a pregnant woman and her two children. I have no idea how it happened except I wanted to get them to safety. I planned for her to live in the foreman's house here, but Doc Bright said she needs to stay in bed rest. And then... well, we shared a hotel room. I haven't touched her, I swear. But I thought by pretending to be married the Kavanagh name would protect her." He ran his fingers through his hair and stared at the horizon.

"You're not married? Why marry her? She's a widow bearing her husband's child. There is nothing wrong about that."

"It sounds simple when you say it." He turned to face his brother. "But she and her husband took in, hid, and sent Negro boys to safety. Slavery might be over, but not everyone follows the law. Men round up these children. They automatically take all the girls, but they only take the healthiest of males. They leave the others in the middle of nowhere to die. Heaven and her husband discovered what was happening and they took in the unwanted boys and hid them until someone else came to take them to safety. Her husband was killed a year ago and she'd been doing it on her own."

"What?"

"The men who round up the children sell them, and they live in her town. They told Heaven to stop, and they got an Indian to have his way with her to punish her. When they saw she was carrying, they laughed. Her shame would be there for everyone to see. When I rode in, though, they were trying to kill her. I'd hate to think what would have happened to Daisy and Tim. They would have been sold most likely."

"Unbelievable! Poor Heaven. Too bad she didn't leave after her husband died."

"She was determined that these boys would continue to have a place to go. I promised to set something up, a place the boys could go while they waited for the next leg to safety. I also told her she'd be safer with the Kavanagh name, and I'd give the baby my name." He shook his head, well aware of the madness of his plan. "It sounded simple. But it's been anything but. She's a strong woman, but I see how much she really needs love… and then the children."

"Just breathe. You have two choices. One, you marry her properly or two, you cut her loose and let her take her chances. I know you're still hurting over that nurse you loved, and I'm sorry about it, but Quinn, you have to decide if it'll be all or nothing. Little Daisy has already proven that you do have a warm heart. The rest is fear, and I don't blame you. I didn't care if I lived or died when Gemma refused my proposal. You know how all that went. But we had a second chance. This could be your chance at real love."

"I need to leave for a few days and get my head straight before I hurt Heaven badly," Quinn insisted. "I need to get Alicia, or whatever her real name was, out of my heart and mind. I can't go back into the house until I come back. I'm sorry to put this on you."

"You do what you have to. I have enough backup. We'll be just fine. The camping equipment is in the barn, and I'll have Dolly bring you some food supplies."

"Thank you, Teagan."

"That's what brothers are for."

CHAPTER NINE

"What do you mean he's gone?" A chill went through her, and she couldn't stop shaking. "He wants me gone, doesn't he? Before he'll come back?" Tears spilled down her face.

"No, he said he needed to get Alicia out of his mind once and for all. He's not one to do things by half measures. For him, it's all or nothing and you scare him. He wants all, but he doesn't want his heart broken again."

"Is there somewhere else I could live? I could work and support me and my children." She felt sick to her stomach.

"Heaven listen to me. He *will* be back. You'll be properly married. Don't worry."

She hung her head. "So, you know about that? We never meant to deceive anyone. It was more for my protection. There are some men, killers who would like to see me dead, and I have my children and the baby coming. If not for the recent gun battle I would have held out. I—a man was killed."

"I can see you're a strong woman. Quinn could have left you in town with some money. He cares, and you two need to have a proper wedding."

Sighing, she shook her head. "I'd rather not talk about it until Quinn gets back. He could change his mind and send us away as soon as the danger is gone."

"You're not going anywhere until your baby is born. No matter what happens, we'll protect you." Teagan gave her a kind smile.

"Thank you. I'm sorry to be such a burden, but could you help me upstairs?"

THREE DAYS LATER, Heaven was busy sewing baby clothes. She already had a pile of diapers hemmed. Sullivan had taken Daisy and Tim fishing, and everything felt relaxing. The ranch was a beautiful place. From the porch, she could see the barn and bunkhouse. The other smaller house must be for the foreman. A big garden was planted on one side of the house while the clothesline was on the other. The front of the porch was lined in flowers swaying in the Texas breeze.

Gemma stepped out with two glasses of water and set them on a table. "Who is that?"

Heaven looked up and sure enough there was a buggy coming their way. A woman held the reins, and she pulled them back as she stopped.

"Is this the Kavanagh Ranch?" a smartly dressed brunette asked.

"Yes." Gemma walked to the buggy and spoke with the woman. When Gemma turned around, she didn't appear happy.

The woman and a small boy exited the buggy and followed Gemma up onto the porch.

"Heaven, this is Alicia Goren and her son Arnold. They are friends of Quinn's. Alicia, Heaven is Quinn's wife."

Heaven nodded to the other woman, but her heart raced.

Alicia was the name of the woman Teagan had said Quinn was trying to forget. "It's nice to meet you."

"When will Quinn be back?" Alicia asked brusquely.

"Probably not today," Gemma told her. "He had ranch business to take care of, and he wasn't sure how long it would take."

"I see. I wanted Quinn to get to know his son. But I'll take my leave."

"No, wait!" Heaven stood. "Is there any way you could stay a few days? I'd hate for Quinn to miss seeing his son."

"We don't have a place to stay, and money is tight. I rented the buggy, and I need to get it back." She peered down at the small boy. "Arnold, are you ready to go?"

"Mama, I want to see cat- catt…"

"Cattle?"

"Yes, Mama, and I want a pony."

Alicia bent and smiled at her son. "Daddy isn't here. We have to go, and hopefully you'll meet him one day."

"Stay," Gemma said. "The foreman's house is empty, and you're welcome to it until Quinn says differently. It needs to be aired out."

Alicia released a sigh. "That would take care of so many of my problems. I can take care of opening the house. I have a few trunks in town I'll need."

"Of course. I'll get a few of the men to drive the buggy and the wagon into town. Let me talk to Teagan." Gemma practically ran to the barn.

"Have a seat," Heaven offered. "I have two children. A boy and a girl. One of the brothers took them fishing."

"Thank you." Alicia sat down and pulled Arnold onto her lap. "It's been hard times, and I wasn't sure where to go. I didn't know Quinn had married."

"How do you know Quinn?" Heaven asked not wanting to know the answer.

"I nursed him. I volunteered at the military hospital. We got to be very close. I left without being able to tell him." A look of sadness entered her eyes. "My father saw how... scarred Quinn is and didn't want someone so damaged for me. He took me away and left me at my aunt's house."

Something didn't ring true, but Heaven couldn't put her finger on which part of the story was a lie. "How old is Arnold?"

Alicia smiled. "Quinn's son is eight years old."

Heaven nodded absently. That child looked to be five years old. Quinn would have to decide whether or not he believed his nurse. Any way it played out it would cause everyone pain. He was free to be with the woman he loved. Heaven could find another place to live and raise her family. Somehow, she'd find a way.

Alicia was lovely. Her skin was perfect. Her green eyes were big and inquisitive. The combination of her green eyes and dark hair was striking. She was so petite, and men liked petite, didn't they? She also had the look of quality to her. Heaven touched her blond hair and felt it listing to the left, ready to fall. Going back to her one braid down her back might be the best thing to do. At least it would look neat that way.

Their clothes couldn't even be compared. Hopefully, Alicia had worn her best dress when planning to see Quinn again. Heaven had never worried much about her clothes. She was proud that she sewed them herself and they weren't torn or faded. But even little Arnold was dressed in a pressed white shirt with brown knickers.

Perhaps she could take the house when Quinn returned and saw the woman he loved. Second chances didn't come around often. Perhaps this was God's way of letting them all know who should be with whom.

Teagan and Shea both met Alicia and then they went to town.

"Alicia, I'm going to open the windows in the house where you'll be staying and take the covers off the furniture. Usually Dolly would help but it's her day off. Would you accompany me and look at the place?"

Alicia turned her head and stared at Heaven, and then she cocked her brow.

"I'm supposed to stay in bed."

"Quinn must be ecstatic."

"This isn't his child. I'm a widow."

Alicia brightened. "So, you and Quinn don't have any children together?"

"No, but he's a wonderful father to my children."

Alicia nodded and stood. "Let's get started." Arnold rubbed his eyes. "I'll find a bed for you to nap on. Come on."

Heaven's heart dropped. Quinn's choice would not be her. She'd have to stay until the baby was born, but once the rest of the family saw the baby, they'd turn their backs on her anyway. She didn't feel so safe and protected now. Tim and Daisy would be heartbroken. They had already lost one father, a father that didn't spend much time with them. Losing Quinn would be devastating, and she had no idea how she'd explain it to them.

A sense of weakness and exhaustion had crept up on her, and she needed to lie down. Her belly hardened in one of the spasms she had been having off and on since the gunfight. She could make it to her room herself. Lying on the sofa with Alicia around wouldn't be resting. Walking inside was easy. It was standing at the bottom of the staircase that brought despair. She put her foot on the bottom step and then the next, moving up one slow step at a time. By the time she lay on the bed, she was exhausted. The spasms didn't stop like they had before, but somehow she fell asleep.

CHAPTER TEN

*H*e was eager to get back to Heaven and the children. It had taken little soul searching to realize he loved them all. Alicia was the past; what he'd had with her had been the first love of a young man. It was a painful lesson. But it was over and best forgotten.

After the baby came, he and his brothers would ride out and take care of the men who had tried to kill her. He also wanted to set up a shelter for the boys wandering Texas.

His thoughts wandered back to the child. A baby… what if he dropped it?

"Come on, Bandit, we're almost home."

Bandit was as keen as he to get home, and the ranch house never looked brighter or more welcoming. One of their wagons stood in front of the foreman's house, and he could see Donnell hauling a trunk inside. "See Bandit? We've only been gone a short while, and the whole world is turned up sided down."

Tim and Daisy were playing with another boy. He didn't see Heaven, but Gemma was on the front porch. He swung down and handed Bandit off to one of the hired men. Quinn was curious what was going on, but he wanted to say hello to Heaven first.

Before he made it to the front porch, a woman almost tackled him. Once he saw her, time moved very slowly, becoming drawn out, as she flung her arms around his neck and pulled his head down for a kiss on the lips. He'd dreamed this very thing night after night, but that was before Heaven. Now that it was happening the way he had yearned for, all he could think of was the strong blond mother who made sure children not her own were safe. Reaching behind his neck he took hold of Alicia's hands and pulled away.

"Alicia? Why are you here?"

"Oh, Quinn…" She tried to step back into his embrace, but he held her at bay. "I wanted you to get to know your son. I didn't know you were married. But I'm staying in your foreman's house for a while so you can see Arnold." She smiled. He remembered that smile; sweet and loving.

"Son? But we never—"

"Oh, but we did." A perfect, pretty pout appeared on her lips. "The doctors had you drugged for the pain, but I always thought you'd remember us being together."

Confusion filled him. He had been out of it a lot, but they hadn't… had they?

"Arnold, come meet your daddy!"

Quinn froze as all three young ones came running his way. Arnold roughly pushed Daisy out of the way and hugged Quinn's waist. Tears rolled down the boy's face. Daisy started to cry, and Quinn disengaged himself from the boy then picked her up and kissed her cheek. Tim stood apart from the rest with a glare on his face. Quinn's heart hurt just gazing at him.

"Tim, I haven't gotten a hug from you," he said gently.

"You have enough people to hug you." Tim ran to the porch and wrapped his arms around Gemma.

"Where is Heaven?"

"She's resting. Apparently being a mother is too much for her." Alicia smiled, but the words sounded catty to Quinn. He hadn't remembered Alicia as being petty like that.

He handed Daisy to Alicia and hurried inside. *What in the blazes is happening?* He took the stairs two at a time then stood outside Heaven's door and watched her sleep. It wasn't a restful sleep. She was moaning, and tears flowed freely. He went to her and sat on the bed. "Heaven, sweetheart, it's me, Quinn."

Her eyes lids fluttered a few times before she was awake. "I had the most awful dream. Did you have a good trip? You had so much to think about, and I was worried."

He took her hand in his and brought it to his lips. He kissed the back of it. "You feel cold."

"I've been having a few pains. I think the baby will come sooner than later."

"Isn't it too early?" He expected to see worry on her face.

"It is, but the pain hasn't increased so I don't know. It's been a… full day." She glanced away from him.

"Yes, I saw them when I arrived. Are you all right?"

"Yes, no, I don't know. You have every right to see your son, and I know you loved Alicia deeply. It's just as well we're not married so you can decide."

"You're not married?"

Quinn turned. "Alicia, who invited you up here? We're having a private discussion."

"I was led to believe you and Heaven were married!" She stepped into the room and glared at Heaven. "Do you know the torment I felt when I was told Quinn *married* you? My heart was broken all for a *lie*?"

Quinn stood. "Alicia that's enough! We both told everyone we're married for reasons of our own." He turned

73

his back on her and sat back down on the bed. "How bad are the pains? Should I send for the doctor?"

"I just need to take my bedrest more seriously. I have done little, but I haven't stayed lying down either. Today has been a bit confusing and wearisome, but I'm trying to stay calm."

Quinn glanced over his shoulder to see they still had company. Irritation flared. "Alicia, would you excuse us and close the door behind you? I don't want to be disturbed, please." His eyes drank her in as she hovered in the doorway. Boy, she looked wonderful, just as he remembered her. Her walnut colored hair wasn't as severely drawn back as it had been in the hospital.

She nodded and closed the door behind her, but her features had taken on a shuttered expression.

Quinn took his boots off and got on the bed. He spooned Heaven and palmed her belly. The baby kicked, and hard. Startled, he yanked his hand away. "What was that?"

"You've felt the baby move before."

"Not like that. It kicked me." He chuckled then put his hand back on her and relaxed.

Her stiffness took a long time to leave, but eventually she seemed tranquil.

"You must be ecstatic Alicia is here. I know you've grieved for her." She put her hand over his. He expected tears. Heaven was a strong woman. "And having a son of your own must be exciting."

"Between you and me, I like Daisy and Tim better, but I haven't had a chance to get to know Arnold."

"You go on and have a good time with your family. I'll be just fine. Don't worry I'm not capable of running off. It's hard to explain but lying here with you, I feel the love of God run through me and brush over me. I have a sense of serenity that I've never had before. Somehow, everything is going to be fine. I'd ask you what you decided while you were away, but things have changed drastically. You had no way of knowing she'd find you. So, I'm not asking for answers now. You need to make the decision that is best for you. The only promise I want you to keep is to build another safe house."

His arms tightened slightly. "Of course, I will. I've been talking to Sullivan about it, and he thinks he knows the right spot. Just... let me hold you and let this moment linger. It feels right to have you in my arms. Any pain now?"

"No, none. You have a calming touch."

They were silent for a time. It was the most peaceful he'd been since forever. He didn't know who Arnold's father was, but his gut told him it wasn't him. He hadn't been healed enough for that before she had left. He'd hear her out though. He had loved her at one time...

"I'll be back up with your supper." He kissed Heaven's cheek before he crawled out of bed. He smiled at her then walked out the door, leaving it open so Daisy and Tim could get to her if they wanted.

Teagan stood at the bottom of the stairs. "I need to talk to you in the office."

Quinn followed him and sat in a chair in front of the desk. "What did you need?"

"I figured you'd need a moment. It's not every day the woman you plan to marry is here and then the love of your life drops back into it."

"It's been shocking," he admitted. "But I made peace with my memories of her. I let her go and was coming home to tell Heaven I have feelings for her and want to be the father of her children. Heaven wants me to see Alicia and see how I feel. She said it was fine if I still love Alicia, that things will work out."

A smile stretched Teagan's lips. "Heaven is a rare woman. You do know that boy can't be eight. Gemma thinks four or five at the most. Besides, when I saw you, you were in no condition to father a child. Your skin was still trying to heal. It hurt when anyone touched you." He angled an assessing look at Quinn. "Or did you somehow manage?"

"No, and I'd like to hear her explanation. She must have hit on hard times if she's here." He couldn't help the smile. "You have to admit she's beautiful."

"It's what's on the inside that shines through, that's real beauty. Don't be fooled by false attractiveness. A pretty face with a conniving heart is dangerous. I feel bad for the children, you know. They all call you daddy."

"I'll talk to Alicia and get the truth. She doesn't have to lie; I'd help her regardless. But I don't love her anymore. The heartbreak has almost disappeared, thanks to Heaven. I'm just sorry the rest of you have a front seat to this drama. If she needs to, I'd like Alicia, or whatever her name is, to stay in the foreman's house until something else is figured out for her." He nodded as a sense of peace settled over him. Heaven was right. "It'll all work out."

CHAPTER ELEVEN

*L*ater that evening, he had Alicia on his arm as they took a walk. What he had initially thought would be easy had turned into a major drama.

"When could we have created Arnold? You know I wasn't capable."

She stopped and gazed at him. "There were plenty of times while you were full of morphine. You don't remember much. I gave you sponge baths and we... Anyway, he is your son and you should be marrying me."

"You shame yourself by saying we... at the hospital. I know I was mad for you, but this doesn't sound true to me. It is so unlike me."

"You were worse than any man who flirted with me. It worked, I liked you best."

Liked? "You... did spend a lot of time with me."

"Yes, I was paid to see you were well taken care of. Teagan donated to the hospital and the doctors had me sit with you. We grew close during that time, and I always enjoyed your company. One of the doctors saw the way you looked at me and sent me to another hospital. It was a huge blow, I had to walk two miles to get there and I was on my feet all day."

"It must have been hard with you being with child. Tell me, where did you go after the baby was born? How long were you able to work at the hospital before the baby came?"

She smiled confidently. He could see it now. The calculating look she cast at him, the perfect smile and starry-eyed expression. She must think him a fool.

"I worked right up to the day he was born. I carried small, so they didn't think I was near my time. I went to work as a housekeeper for a doctor. Dr. Beal was a nice man. He didn't mind that I had Arnold. He worked much of the time."

"THAT'S A RELIEF. I'm glad you were safe. I looked for you, but I couldn't find you. Alicia Goren didn't exist." And how would she explain that? "I guess I was also worried why you left. How long did you work for Dr. Beal?"

"About two years. Then he married, and his wife didn't want any competition, so I left and found another position. I worked for a banker Mr. Parma. He was very fussy about everything, and he didn't like that I sometimes went to lunch with Dr. Beal. He didn't understand our friendship. My next position was working as a companion for an elderly woman. She died a month ago, and here we are."

"A colorful life."

She smiled. "Yes, that is a perfect way of putting it. I know Arnold is small for his age, but he's sturdy. I knew you'd take us in."

"I see." He had nothing else to say. He'd send telegrams to the two doctors, and if he could get her name from Alicia without raising suspicions, he would contact the elderly woman's family. He'd get to the bottom of it all. He stared at her, and she tilted her head, awaiting a kiss. There was a time he had seen those lips as perfectly shaped and oh, how he had longed to kiss her. But now, out of those lips lies spilled.

He stepped away.

"I'll walk you home. Please be kind to Heaven. She needs to rest. She's had a hard time of it. And don't go anywhere without telling someone. We might have some gunmen wanting revenge coming our way." He stopped at the door to the foreman's house. "Good night."

Dolly came out. "He's ready for bed but he wanted to see his mother." She said nothing else, just stalked to the ranch house.

"I'll take my leave. Have a pleasant evening." He didn't wait for a reply. He needed to make a timeline and he needed to do some thinking. *Lord please guide me in this.*

HEAVEN WATCHED as Alicia tilted her head waiting for a kiss then turned from the window. It would be too painful to watch. Her heart hurt. She loved Quinn. It was a disgraceful thought; her husband hadn't been dead all that long.

Now she looked at herself in the mirror. Her whole body was bloated, and she was fat. Alicia was so pretty and petite. Arnold was not Quinn's child; he couldn't be for he was far too young. But it wasn't up to her to say anything. He had loved that woman so much it almost destroyed him. Was he falling for her again? They'd walked arm in arm in the moonlight. It was hard to see, but she was pretty sure Alicia had been smiling.

Heaven sighed. Alicia wasn't the intruder. She was. Quinn didn't love her like a man should. She needed to be done with this sham of a marriage. It would only make him look bad if people thought him married but courting another. He couldn't have known he'd ever see her again, and he had been planning to settle for her and the children.

Her heart hurt much more than she imagined it would. Yes, she'd have her child here and then she'd find her way. Maybe she could be a mail-order bride. But what would happen to the child she carried? People were cruel to half-breeds. She'd find a safe place where the baby would be accepted, she vowed. It just wouldn't be here.

In the meantime, the bed looked inviting, and she lay down and was soon joined by Tim and Daisy.

"Is that boy going to live here?" Tim asked in a surly voice.

He lay on one side while Daisy lay on the other. She kissed both their heads and pulled them close to her. "I think he'll probably be here for a very long time."

"Daddy doesn't want us anymore." Tim turned his head away but not before she saw his tears.

"It's not that. I'm sure he loves you both very much. He thought Alicia was... dead. He loved her with all his heart, and her being back has changed things. We won't be leaving for a while yet, so don't worry."

"I lub Dada." Heaven didn't know what to tell Daisy and tears ran down her face too.

"It'll be just fine. We've been on our own before, and we did just fine."

"No, not really. We were just waiting for those men to come and kill us."

Heaven sighed. Tim was too perceptive.

"There are other places to live where there aren't bad men. I know it hurts, but we are strong and brave. We can make it through this and remember God is always with us."

Tim wiped away his tears and nodded, but Daisy wouldn't be consoled. "Honey, your real daddy was a brave man, and he was shot. He would have stayed with you forever if he could have. He loved you both very much. He was proud of you both."

Daisy's cries quieted as she listened to Heaven, but as Heaven's words slowed, the child went back to cries of deep, heartfelt pain. Daisy was too young to have her heart broken again. It wasn't fair, but life was like that.

Footsteps sounded in the hallway, and Teagan walked into the room. He scooped Daisy into his arms. "Your crying makes me sad."

"I'm saddest. I never want another daddy."

Teagan's eyes watered as he glanced at Heaven. He rocked Daisy back and forth. She buried her face in his neck as she continued to cry out her grief.

Heaven had tried to be courageous, but a sob bubbled up and it took everything to be quiet. It wasn't Quinn's fault. It was just their fate. Alicia seemed nice enough. Heaven wasn't the first woman to be jilted for another. Her eyes must be raw and red. Swallowing over and over helped her to pull herself back together. She hugged, Tim but he didn't want to be hugged. She let him be.

Daisy stopped crying for a moment and Heaven glanced up. Quinn stood in front of Teagan with his arms out for Daisy. She practically jumped into Quinn's arms, but her cries became worse. She would cry herself sick. Teagan quietly left the room.

"Perhaps I should put Tim and Daisy to bed now," Heaven said, her voice raspy. "They'll be fine. One thing guaranteed in life is change. When one door is closed, God makes sure there is another door that opens."

She started to haul herself out of bed.

"No, stay and rest. I'm going to show these two the stars. We'll be gone a while so no worrying, all right?"

She nodded, unable to find her voice. He was such a good

man. He gathered up a quilt and put a hand out for Tim to take, and the three of them left.

CHAPTER TWELVE

Quinn hadn't thought out how the children would react. He'd told these two he'd be their dad. He loved them. How was this all supposed to work? He had no plans to marry Alicia. She didn't know what truth meant. Had she ever?

He walked them into an empty pasture and spread out the quilt. Then he lay down in the middle. "Come join me."

Daisy snuggled right up to him while Tim lay down but not as close as usual.

"Look up at all those stars. And over there that's the moon. It—"

Daisy planted her chin on his chest and stared into his eyes. "Dada no lub me."

It felt as though his heart was being ground to dust by a boot heel.

"I do love you, Daisy, and Tim, I love you too."

"Mama?" She cried. Daisy glared at him.

"I love all three of you. I need to straighten a few things around, but I don't want you to worry."

"Is our mama a bad woman?" Tim asked.

"No, she isn't. Where did you hear that?"

"One night a bunch of men pushed the door in. Daisy and me hid, but they grabbed Mama. She screamed and cried a lot and they told her no one would want her now. Is that what's wrong? You don't want her?" Tim swallowed hard.

"Your mother is the bravest, most loving woman I know. What those men said isn't true. Your mother is a good woman. You're going to have a brother or sister soon."

"A half-breed bastard." Tim nodded.

Quin's next breath stalled in his throat. "Where did you hear words like that?" he choked out. "Those men?"

"Yes, sir."

"Never use those words again," he said gently. "They are hateful words. God loves all his children. Every child. Sometimes people say mean things to people different from them. The baby might have a different color skin or eyes than you two, but it'll still be your brother or sister."

"Lub baby?" Daisy's earnest stare was unnerving him.

"Yes, I do and I do love both of you as my own. Never doubt that." Suddenly, he had to get back. "We'll do the stars another night. Your mama might get worried."

"But you told her not to worry," Tim reminded him.

"I did." He shrugged, trying to remain nonchalant. "But women tend to fuss and worry."

Tim nodded as if he understood then got up and helped to fold the quilt.

Quinn could feel Alicia's stare as they walked past the house where she was staying. He led the children into the ranch house. "Let's get ready as quickly as we can so we can give Mama a kiss goodnight."

Tim raced up the steps, and Daisy tried hard to follow. After a moment, Quinn picked her up and raced her to the top. "Can you dress yourself?"

Daisy put her finger in her mouth and looked at him. He

hugged her to him and kissed her cheek. "Let's find your nightgown."

By the time he and Daisy walked into Heaven's bedroom, Tim was already there smiling.

"I'm quick, aren't I?"

"You sure are," Quinn assured him. "We hit a few snags, but I think we got it right." He put Daisy on the bed next to Heaven.

Heaven chuckled and gave him a beautiful smile.

"Kiss Mama."

Heaven kissed Daisy a few times until she laughed.

Tim lifted his cheek toward her and she gave him a kiss too.

Gemma came in. "I hope I'm not intruding, I know a good bedtime story, but I can't find Teagan. Maybe I could tell it to you two?"

Tim shot out of bed, and Daisy was waving her arms toward Gemma. Gemma took her and closed the door behind her.

"That was nice of her," Heaven said. "So, did they get an education about the stars?"

Quinn took off his boots and climbed on the bed. This time he kissed her cheek and laid her head on his chest, pulling her as close as possible.

"No, we looked at a few and then they had a lot of questions. I've handled this whole thing badly, but I wanted to know what Alicia had to say. I know Arnold isn't mine, but I felt if she was in some sort of trouble, I would have liked to help." He heaved a sigh. "But by doing so, I broke those little ones' hearts. I never meant to hurt them… or you. I hope it's all right with you, but I told them that I am their daddy and the baby's daddy too."

She said nothing.

"I should have checked with you first."

"No, I'm trying not to be a watering pot. I feel like I've been crying all day, but I think maybe I'm cried out. Quinn, Alicia is beautiful, and she has a nice figure, she's not fat like me."

He laughed. "You, my love, are carrying a child. My child. If you agree, I'd like to be wed before the baby arrives."

"What's the catch?" Her voice was so raspy.

"No catch. I just happen to like you." He rubbed her back. "Let me tell you, Heaven, I never planned to smile at a woman again. I was set to live the rest of my life single. There are too many people around here to be alone. The first time I saw you standing on your front porch with your rifle aimed at those men, I knew you were special. I tried, the Lord knows I tried to just be a friend who was passing through."

She sniffed. "I'm sorry my problems kept you with me."

"That wasn't what was wrong, what kept me from leaving." A chuckle slipped out. "It was you and your two rascals. I'm proud to know such a brave woman. You are sweet and giving and you love. I see your love when you look at your children. Even though you were attacked, you still love the child you carry. You're ready to let me go because you think it'll make me happy."

"Will it? Will it make you happy?" She lifted her head from his solid chest and stared into his eyes.

He smiled wider than he had in a very long time. "No. There is only one thing in this world that will make me happy. I would be extremely happy if you would marry me for real."

Her face glowed, but her forehead creased. "Are you sure? Alicia was the love of your life. Quinn, we don't have to make such a big life decision now. I'd rather take our time than live in regret later." She held up her hand. "We can take it slow, Quinn. We need to weigh every aspect. I have no idea where we'd live or if you have other plans than to stay on the ranch. This house is really Gemma's domain. After a while it would —" She sighed again. "There is so much to think on. You need to talk with Alicia a bit more. I'm not worried about the future. I'm sure God will provide." She put her head back down and snuggled closer.

CHAPTER THIRTEEN

*Q*uinn stretched as he woke. He'd slept beside Heaven all night. He hadn't planned on it since most knew they weren't married. He turned to see if she was awake, but she wasn't there. Where in tarnation was she? She was supposed to stay in bed. He scowled and then rubbed his hand over his face.

He put his boots back on and clomped down the stairs. A loud moan came from outside. He rushed to the porch, and spotting her on the ground, he fell to his knees. "Heaven, what is it? The baby? How long have you been out here?" He gathered her into his arms. "Let's get you back into the house." Her skin was so very pale. She moaned again.

Quinn lifted her and struggled to his feet. He glanced up and saw Alicia sitting on her front steps, just watching. He gritted his teeth. Whatever was up, he didn't have time to wonder about it now. He hurried inside and up the stairs. Gently, he settled Heaven on the bed.

Dolly and Gemma suddenly appeared. "I have water starting to boil and I started gathering things we'll need,"

Dolly said taking charges. "Gemma, I'll need the oilcloths and sheets stored in the room you sleep in, in the wardrobe."

"I know where they are." Gemma ran out of the room.

Dolly stripped everything off the bed except for the sheet Heaven lay upon. She took the oilcloth from Gemma. "Quinn, I'll need you to lift her while I put this on the bed to protect it and then a few other sheets."

Quinn lifted Heaven while the two women went to work. They were quick, and he placed Heaven in the middle of the bed. "Should I go for the doctor?"

"Don't leave me!" Heaven reached out and grabbed his hand.

"I'll send someone," Teagan said. He yawned and patted down the hair that was sticking up on end.

Quinn sat near the top of the bed near Heaven's head. He'd helped birth many animals, but this was too different. Each time Heaven groaned; she squeezed his hand. He wasn't sure if his fingers would all be in one piece by the time the baby came.

Gemma handed him a cold, wet cloth. "Wipe her brow and make her comfortable."

He wanted to laugh. Comfortable? That probably wasn't going to happen soon. He took the cloth and blotted Heaven's forehead and then her face and neck. This time when she screamed and squeezed his hand, he wasn't ready and he winced. She had a strong grip.

"I haven't even thought about names for the baby," she wailed.

"That can be done after." Quinn smiled at her.

"It won't be long now," Dolly announced.

Gemma had laid out the scissors and thread and a threaded needle on a clean towel. She also had a pile of towels.

"How long were you outside?" he asked.

"Too long," she screamed.

"It's fine, your mama will be just fine," Sullivan could be heard saying.

"See if Alicia can make breakfast!" Dolly yelled.

"Are you ready, Heaven? One more push should do it."

Heaven nodded to Dolly and pushed. It all happened so fast. One minute Heaven groaned and her face was turning red, and the next the baby was born and Heaven sagged back onto the bed and let go of his hand. The baby gave a lusty cry, and it looked like they were cleaning the child.

"Girl or boy?" he asked.

"It's a boy. A beautiful boy," Gemma told them, her eyes bright with unshed tears.

Dolly put her hand on Quinn's shoulder. "Why don't you wait outside? We want to get Heaven cleaned up and be sure everything is fine and change the bedding and such."

He starred into Heaven's tearful blue eyes. Leaning over he kissed her hard on the lips. "We have a son," he whispered before he stood up.

Her smile made him feel so loved, so adored. If only he could stay and bask in it, but Dolly had already ordered him to leave. She would shoo him out any second.

"I'll check on the other two." He closed the door behind him and then leaned against the wall feeling exhausted. *Thank you, Lord, for this blessing.* Quinn pushed off the wall, drew a deep breath, and headed downstairs.

His boots had just hit the bottom step when Tim and Daisy came running. After stepping away from the stairs he hunkered down with his arms open. The two children raced to him and hugged him.

"You have a brother."

Daisy pushed at him until he let them go.

"What's wrong?"

"She wanted a sister," said Tim, laughing. "I told her it would be a brother, but she insisted on a sister," Tim said as he shook his head.

"Just think, Daisy, you're still the only girl around. You know everyone adores you. They'll want to hold the baby, of course, but I think your smile is such that a person can't look away."

Daisy smiled. "I'm bootifil." She grabbed Quinn around his neck kissing his cheek and choking him at the same time.

"When can we see our mama?" Tim sounded impatient.

"Let's eat while she gets changed into a fresh nightgown." Quinn managed to pry Daisy's hand from his neck, and he held her as he stood. "What are we having?"

"Whatever I'm making!" Teagan yelled from the kitchen.

Quinn smiled and set Daisy down. Teagan walked to him and gave him one heck of a hug. "Congratulations, Quinn."

"Thank you. I'm a little overwhelmed, but I'm sure it will pass."

"I need to flip the flapjacks."

Quinn gazed at his brothers' happy faces. Alicia and Arnold were nowhere to be seen. "I thought Alicia was making breakfast."

Murphy laughed. "She would only make breakfast for you and her and her boy. No one else."

Quinn blinked twice. "What?"

Fitzpatrick started laughing too. "I guess she doesn't know what a family is."

"Maybe we scare her?" Angus said.

"Where did she go? If she was going to be that way, why didn't she just stay at the house?" Quinn shook his head.

Alicia was so different from what he remembered. She was still beautiful, but what had happened to offering caring and kindness and love? He'd been such a fool not to see how selfish she truly was. Had he really thought they'd be married? Her explanation of why she'd left wasn't quite believable. He had checked with the other hospitals, but no one had ever heard of her... unless maybe she changed her name again. And he never had been able to get her to give him the name of the elderly woman she had worked for. Another dead end. So why him and why now? There must be some other fools she could force a son on. He took a deep breath, struggling with his emotions. He needed to remember that Arnold was an innocent in all this. Was she wanted or running from the law? Maybe she already had a husband. If only she'd just tell the truth, he'd be willing to help.

"What did you name the baby?" Sullivan asked.

"Heaven needs to figure that out. If she wants help, she'll ask for it. Right now, she just needs a rest. I'm sure you'll all be able to see the baby in a little while."

Quinn smiled as he watched Tim and Daisy eat flapjacks. They'd need some cleaning up before they saw their mama. A lump formed in his throat. Children were a lot of responsibility and he hoped with God's help he'd be able to do right by them.

The front door opened, and little Arnold ran into the kitchen and wrapped his arms around Quinn's legs.

"Well how ya doing, bud? Did your mom make you something to eat?"

Alicia walked in and gave him a bright smile. "Of course, I fed him. We came by to see the new baby. Where is it?" She pretended to look around.

"The baby is with his mama. I was just about to take Tim and Daisy up to see her and the baby."

"Aren't you forgetting someone?" She stared at him.

"Oh no, he did not." Dolly came down the stairs. "Heaven asked to see Tim, Daisy, and Quinn."

"But surely…"

Dolly shook her head. "That baby is of no relation to you or your child. I'm sure Arnold can see the baby later. Now I will get a cup of tea and put my feet up for a while." Dolly hustled into the kitchen.

Tim and Daisy ran toward Quinn. "Wait, let me see your hands." Both children put their hands out for Quinn to see. "Looks good to me, let's go. Now, I want you to remain calm and speak softly while we're up there visiting your mother and the new baby. Your mama is probably very tired, so we won't stay long." He took both of them by the hand and led them up the stairs.

Quinn opened the bedroom door and stared. Daisy and Tim went into the room, but Quinn felt transfixed by the most beautiful sight he'd ever seen. Heaven was feeding their son and the look of joy on her face was one he'd never seen before.

"Quinn are you going to stand there or are you coming in?" Heaven asked with a chuckle.

Quinn stepped into the room and closed the door behind him. "How are you feeling?"

"Tired, but it's a good tired. I worried so about this baby, and here he is just perfect. It looks as though I won't be able to go anywhere for a while. I don't want you to think you are saddled with us. I've always been capable, so I'm not afraid."

"He wrinkly," Daisy blurted.

"He sure is little. I guess we won't be playing tag with him anytime soon," Tim added.

"Babies seem to grow fast." Heaven patted the bed. "Come sit next to me so you can get a better look at your brother."

Quinn helped Daisy onto the bed next to her mama. "He's a handsome boy that's for sure. I'm thankful that you are both fine."

"Are you his daddy?" Tim asked with his eyes narrowed.

Quinn smiled and gazed into Heaven's eyes. He was surprised to see a speck of a question in them. She certainly wasn't very trusting.

"Of course I'm his daddy, just like I'm your daddy and I'm Daisy's daddy. I think we make a nice family. What do you think?"

Tim seemed to mull his answer over in his mind. Finally, he nodded. "Well you are a good daddy. You know how to stop Daisy from crying, and you have lots of brothers who like to fish. Plus, I can't wait to learn to ride a horse. But best of all, Mama likes you."

Quinn had to blink back the moisture that formed in his eyes. "Why, thank you, that was quite the endorsement." He gazed at Heaven. "Have you thought of a name for this little one?"

Tim brightened. "I like the name Jasper. I once had a turtle named Jasper. Or how about Bandit? It's been a good name for the horse. Oh, I've got it let's name him Quinn number two!"

Heavens lips twitched as she locked gazes with Quinn. "Those are very good suggestions Tim, I will take them into consideration. What about you Daisy? Do you have any suggestions?"

"Cave and Baby."

"Those are good suggestions too," Heaven said as she nodded.

"What were *you* thinking of naming him?" Quinn asked.

"I just don't know. I was thinking maybe Owen. It was my father's name. What do you think?" She'd finished nursing the baby and was trying to get him to burp.

Quinn sat on the bed and put his arms out for the baby boy. "Owen is a good name. I like it." He smiled when Heaven put Owen into his arms. Everything about the baby was tiny, from his nose to his toes and all the parts in between. He didn't look Indian, at least not yet, and Quinn wasn't going to mention that. "He is a little miracle. Heaven, we are blessed, and I don't want to hear about you leaving. We are a family and families stay together."

She nodded, but she didn't look convinced.

CHAPTER FOURTEEN

*I*t had been three-and-a-half weeks, and Heaven was at her wits' end. She didn't begrudge Arnold one bit, but Alicia was pushing her and she didn't like it. When was she going to leave? Had she even told Quinn why she was here? Alicia acted as though she hated Owen, and she didn't hide it. She never crossed the line, but she came close. Alicia always had an outing planned for herself, Arnold, Quinn, Tim, and Daisy. She kept telling Heaven that she needed to rest, which meant staying home alone.

There were plenty of times Quinn just said no, but there were also many times when the children begged him to go. Alicia had taken to letting them in on her plans before putting them to Quinn so they would grow excited at the prospects of these outings. And Heaven couldn't help herself. She kept looking for signs that Quinn was attracted to Alicia. He hadn't mentioned marriage since before the baby was born. But Heaven wasn't without allies. Dolly, Gemma, Teagan, and Sullivan all wanted Alicia to leave. Fitzpatrick had gone into town a couple of weeks back and sent out telegrams trying to find out who Alicia really was. So far there had been no answers.

Heaven no longer shared a bed with Quinn, and every night was lonely and oh so cold. He lingered each evening, and they talked, but eventually they had to say good night. It was strange almost as though the topic of Alicia was to be avoided. Heaven was waiting for Quinn to bring it up. Maybe he didn't want the special feeling they had when they were alone to be interrupted.

Owen was doing nicely. He was such a good baby, and he loved Quinn. If she couldn't get him to stop fussing, Quinn could. It was a joy to see Quinn with her children.

Quinn stuck his head outside and asked if she needed anything.

"No, I'm just enjoying the sunrise in peace. Why don't you grab your coffee and join me?"

Quinn gave her a lazy grin and nodded before he closed the door.

Out of the corner by she thought she saw someone running with the rifle. She looked again but there was no movement. A chill went through her and she had a bad feeling. Quickly, she opened the door and got inside locking it behind her.

She put the baby in the cradle and grabbed one of the rifles from over the fireplace mantel. As she was checking to see if it was loaded Quinn spotted her.

"Is there something going on that I should know about?"

"I think I saw someone running through the woods with a rifle. I couldn't find him again, but I have a feeling he's out there. I always feel better with a rifle in my hands. I will keep watch out the front window."

Quinn nodded, already grabbing another rifle from over the mantel. "I'll get Teagan and the rest of the boys. I trust your intuition. Make sure you stay down and don't make yourself a target."

She crawled to the window and looked out from the very bottom corner. They had come for her. She just knew it. And if anyone got hurt, it would be her fault. She stood, took a deep breath and walked to the door. She was just about to unlock it when Teagan came into the room.

"Whoa, what do you think you're doing?"

"I'm doing what I must to protect my family. This isn't the first time I've met these people on a porch. I'm not afraid of them anymore." Her bravado was undermined by the quiver in her voice.

"I'll take that rifle away if I have to," Teagan threatened. "You have children who need you, depend on you. I can't let anything happen to you. Why don't you go upstairs with Gemma, Dolly and the children?"

"I'm good with the rifle."

Quinn came into the room and scowled at her. "Owen is down here he could get hurt. I know you think this is your fight but honey we're your family now."

Before she could answer him, the rest of the Kavanagh brothers piled in, each collecting ammunition for their weapons. They were a small army; they really didn't need her. She went to Quinn and handed him her rifle. Next, she reached up and pulled his head down so she could kiss him. It was the longest kiss they'd ever shared.

Taking her rifle back, she grabbed up Owen and went flying up the stairs. No sooner had she put Owen into his cradle, than Quinn yelled out that all was clear. Heaven exchanged troubling glances with Gemma.

"Heaven, if you could come down here please, it would be most appreciated," Quinn yelled up the stairs.

With the rifle still in hand Heaven walked down. Some of the Kavanagh brothers had glints in their eyes. Then she saw him, the man who had attacked her, the man who had fathered her child. Her first instinct was to spit in his face, but she had been raised better than that. She quickly went to Quinn's side and looked up at him questions racing through her mind but refusing to be put into words.

She welcomed Quinn's arm as he put it over her shoulder.

"This is him, isn't it?" Quinn asked.

Heaven couldn't stop her body from shaking as she nodded. She stared into the Indian's black eyes, afraid to know why he was there.

"My son is fine, yes?" He spoke quietly. "You have a nice home. I just wanted to be sure he was fine. No one will bother you again. You have my word."

Not knowing what to do, she nodded in silence and held onto Quinn's hand. Somehow, she expected an apology, but soon realized there would not be one.

"Yes, *my son* is well," she finally said, allowing a bit of defiance to come through.

"I'll go now. You won't see me again. Raise my son to be brave and honorable." He walked out the door.

Quinn took the rifle out of Heaven's hand and set it down. Next, he took her into his arms and held her close. "I don't think we'll see him again. I believe him. It's good to know we won't have to look over our shoulders for those men anymore."

"He knows where we live," murmured Heaven, unable to shake off a sense of apprehension. "Do you really think he'll stay away?"

"He could have brought the others if he wanted to. But he came alone. We'll have our men be on guard, but I have a feeling he'll keep the others, the bad men away." Quinn nodded in reassurance as his voice grew stronger in conviction. "He looked right proud when I told him it was a boy. Something in him seemed to... care. Even if we tried to go after him now, we'd never find him. I think we can breathe easier."

Dolly and Gemma poured coffee as if it was just another day, and Heaven calmed in the wake of the normal routine.

"I'll have breakfast rustled up for you all right quick," Dolly said with a smile.

Quinn seated Heaven and gave her shoulder a slight squeeze.

"Oh, my children! I left the children upstairs," Heaven said as she started to stand. How could she have forgotten them?

"I'll take care of them," Gemma offered. A shy smile lit her features. "After all, I need to practice."

She was up the stairs before it sank in. Heaven turned to Quinn. "She's with child," she murmured, and she and Quinn exchanged happy smiles.

The room filled with cheers and words of congratulations as the brothers surrounded Teagan, with hugs and a few good-natured slaps on the back.

Dolly rushed in from the kitchen with tears in her eyes. She went to Teagan and hugged him for a very long time. Finally, she let go. "I never thought to see the day... I just am so happy... Imagine Teagan is going to be a father." With a sniff and a dash of her hand across her tear-streaked cheeks, she scurried back into the kitchen, mumbling something about burned eggs.

It was turning out to be a fine morning indeed, Heaven decided with a sigh of contentment. There was only one person on the ranch who could ruin things, and the door burst open just as that thought crossed Heaven's mind.

Alicia raced into the house shrieking about being scalped by an Indian. She stalked over to Heaven and stood toe to toe with her, pointing her finger right in Heaven's face. "This is your fault. Don't think you pulled the wool over my eyes. I know that baby up there—" she jerked her head toward the ceiling, indicating the upstairs "—isn't Quinn's, and it's not your dead husband's either—if you ever had a husband in the first place."

Heaven stiffened and narrowed her eyes at the other woman but otherwise refused to show any reaction.

Shaking with emotion, Alicia continued to spew venom. "I just knew it. Did the Indian want to take the boy with him? That would be the best thing to do." Alicia stared hard at Heaven.

"I'm afraid you have everything wrong, Alicia," said Quinn, his voice calm and quiet but with a hard edge underneath. "That is my son upstairs. I don't want to hear another word about it. Do you understand?"

The tension in the room grew. If anyone should go, it should be Alicia. How long was the blasted woman staying anyway? Heaven sighed, supposing that would be up to Quinn.

"Where's Arnold?" Sullivan asked. "You didn't leave him behind, did you?"

"I figured he'd be safer in the house." She subjected them all to scathing glances and then, with a huff, she trounced out.

Heaven was glad she was gone, but it still didn't answer her question of when she was leaving for good. Did she dare broach the subject to Quinn? After she finished her coffee, she went upstairs to see the children and to give Gemma a great big hug.

"I'm so excited for you, and of course Teagan," she gushed. "How long have you known? How have you been feeling?"

Gemma chuckled. "I've known for a couple months, but I just told Teagan a week ago, and now you all know. Mornings are unpredictable, I'm afraid. Some days I'm sick to my stomach, and other days I'm fine. Just very excited and eager to become a mother."

"You will be a great one," Heaven assured her with one more hug.

The rest of the day was quiet, but Heaven couldn't seem to put aside her uneasiness. She spent a great part of the day on the porch staring into the woods. Why would that Indian give up his child so easily? Did he not have a family he could take the baby to? Quinn had said he seemed to care... Then how could he walk away? *Had* he walked away? In many ways she was now more frightened than she had been while living alone with her children.

The front door opened, and without looking, she knew it was Quinn.

He stepped outside and with slow steps she barely heard, he came up behind her and wrapped his loving arms around her. He said nothing for the longest time, and she leaned back knowing with certainty that she loved him.

"You've looked pensive and anxious all day. Is there anything I can say or do to ease your fear?"

"No, there isn't." She sighed and leaned against him. "I wish I could just take it all at face value, but I can't. I do draw comfort in the fact that what you have equates to a small army. Your brothers are quick to take action."

Quinn chuckled and gave her a squeeze. "I have never seen anyone as quick as you."

She took a deep breath and shook her head. "I know what he's capable of. I know how hurtful and torturous he can be. There's no conscience behind his cold eyes. I don't think he'll be back while Owen is young, but I have the feeling he'll be back. I don't trust that man. I've been uneasy all day. All I want is my serenity back."

Quinn turned her in his arms and swooped down for a kiss. The kiss was very gentle at first and then she could feel his need. He might think he wanted her, and the Lord knew she wanted him. But he needed to figure out how he felt about her and how he felt about Alicia. Quinn loved her, she knew, but he might love Alicia more. It was going to be hard to wait-and-see. For her, marriage was the only thing that would ease her fears.

And speaking of the devil, Alicia had been on her porch watching and now she was on her way to them.

Heaven shook her head and backed toward the door. "Quinn, I'm not up for her tonight. I'm going inside."

Quinn eased his hold, but before he let her go, he pulled her back for one more kiss. She barely made it inside before having to acknowledge Alicia.

CHAPTER FIFTEEN

*Q*uinn nodded to Alicia. "Long day."

"It has been, and very worrisome." Alicia smiled into his eyes. "But I have faith in you and your brothers that nothing will happen to us. I've never felt so protected before."

What was she angling at now? "The Kavanagh ranch is about as safe as any place around."

"Yes… I can see why you brought Heaven and the children here." She tilted her head. "You always had a chivalrous calling. It's one of the things I fell in love about you."

He didn't want to have this conversation with her. Ever. "Alicia, I think—"

"Are you and Heaven sharing a bed?" she blurted.

"Of course not." Taken aback by her directness, Quinn scowled at her.

"Well, what am I supposed to think? Why would you need a pretend marriage? The only reason I can think of is that you compromised her. Is that why you're thinking of marrying her?" A light danced in her eyes. "If you are thinking of marriage, I think you'd consider me too. After all, I took care of you for months and we grew close, very close. I had imagined that it would be you and me walking down the aisle one day. It's just hard to watch you play daddy and husband to Heaven and her children when there's me and—"

"I'm not playing anything," he insisted. "It's you who came here pretending things. I've included your son in everything we do. You're the one who told him I was his father, and you must be the one to explain why I'm not." He walked to the railing on the porch and held onto it until his knuckles turned white. It was a clear beautiful sky, and Heaven was right. Some serenity would be wonderful.

He turned and crossed his arms in front of him as he tried to think of what to say. "You know, you're right. We became very close, you and me. I considered you the love of my life, but you left. And when I came home, I mourned you. I mourned you up into the day I met Heaven. My heart was so broken. I laid in the hospital for weeks hoping you'd come back. No one knew where you were, and then it was discovered that your name is not your name."

Her sharp intake of breath was her only reaction.

"But fool that I am I couldn't bring myself to doubt you," he went on, raking his gaze over her,. "When I was better, I spent months looking for you. Months that I could have been here helping with the ranch. I was different when I came home. Not because of the war, but because of you. You could have found me at any time. After all, you're here now, aren't you? Teagan knew where I was for the most part and he could've gotten word to me. I feel deceived and cheated, and most of all stupid to think we'd be together. And you haven't been truthful since you came here. I know because I tried to verify your story by writing to some folks. No one knew you then, and no one knows you now. You'd best get back to your boy." He gestured toward the little house where she was staying. "I have a lot of thinking to do." He stepped toward the door.

"Quinn, wait!" Her tone held a note of desperation. "Please. I-I'm so sorry it turned out that way. What I told you was the truth except... it wasn't a doctor who saw the way you looked at me, it was my father. He had forbidden me to work at the hospital, so I used a different name. But he found me there one day, and he was livid. Walking through the fires of hell would have been easier than listening to what he would do to you." Tears streamed down her cheeks. "Alicia is my middle name. My real name is Lauren Alicia Gregory. I never meant to deceive you, but I wasn't using my real name. I feared if I told you, you would let it slip to someone who would know my father."

She reached in his direction as though to seek solace in his embrace, but he stepped back, shaking his head.

"Taking care of you and being with you were the best times of my life, and when I could come out here, I prayed and prayed that you hadn't married yet. God granted my prayer. Don't you see? That's why you aren't married!"

Had she always seemed to border on insane like this?

"I just wish I had gotten here a couple years sooner," she said more quietly. Then she gave him a sad smile, turned and walked away.

Quinn watched her leave then sat down on the step and buried his face in his hands. He wasn't sure whether he could believe Alicia—or Lauren. He had loved her beyond anything he'd ever experienced before. But that had been then and this was now. Slowly he raised his head and stared at the little house where she'd disappeared. She hadn't even bothered to deny that Arnold wasn't his child. While he'd known it, somehow this lack of denial became a confirmation to him. It was true she had taken good care of him while he'd been near death, and he probably *would* have died without her. She had given him the will to live. Funny thing, he had always thought love was forever. But it wasn't. How naïve he'd been. He looked out at the sky again, wondering if he was any wiser now.

If he went with Alicia, she knew what she was getting, she'd seen his scars. Heaven hadn't. She didn't know how ugly and deformed the thick scar tissue made him. One look at that mess, and he could lose her forever. Most women would run, and he couldn't blame them. Heck, he didn't even like looking at himself. His severe burn scars always made him wince to look at and often gave him physical distress. Maybe he should've told Heaven about it earlier. It wasn't something that would come up in conversation, though, and he wasn't sure what to say. He didn't want her pity, yet he didn't want her to look at him in horror either.

He chuckled sadly and looked across the land to the horizon, the grazing cattle, the scrub brush leading to forest, the sun painting the sky in reds and oranges as it sank. Everything around him had some sort of beauty to it; everything but him. Had Alicia ever really cared for him? There was still something about her that wasn't truthful, but he wasn't sure what it was. More likely was the fact that she didn't love him at all and never had. Did little Arnold's father even know he existed? Oh yes, he'd done some thinking, and now he had a new set of questions for her. He just wasn't looking forward to the answers.

And he was just like Alicia, part of him acknowledged, by keeping things from Heaven. Heaven's opinion of him mattered a lot. He needed to tell her about his scars, and he needed to tell her soon. He just dreaded the whole thing, but it would be better coming from him than from Alicia.

AT THE KNOCK on her door, Heaven simply said, "Come in."

As soon as the words were out, she knew it might be a mistake. She needed to check who she was inviting into her room from now on. But the door opened and Quinn entered. He looked so sad is if he'd just lost his best friend. He gave her a small smile and then walked to the window. What was he looking at that was so interesting?

"I don't think it's proper for you to be in here, is it? I don't want to stir up anything with your family, I really like them." Then she cringed. She hadn't intended for the words to come out so harsh.

His back stiffened, and he turned around and came toward the bed. "Mind if I sit next to you?"

Her heart softened. She'd never deny him any reasonable request. "Of course not. Quinn, what's wrong? You know you can tell me anything."

He gazed at her for a moment and nodded. "But what if I told you something that made you hate me?"

Her eyes widened. "Unless you were just downstairs kissing Alicia and planning to lie about it, I can't think of anything that would make me hate you. You are a fine man, a good man, and I believe in you."

His Adam's apple bobbed up and down a few times, and then he sighed. "I was injured in the war. I know I told you about it, but I just never let on the extent of my injuries."

"Quinn, I already know what you're going to say and that's just fine. My husband never made it a good experience. In fact, it was mostly painful and…" Humiliating, or so she had thought until Owen's father had gotten ahold of her. She shrugged. "So if you can't… you know, it's all right."

Quinn's lips twitched and his eyes filled with mirth. "I don't have problems in that area. In fact, I know I can do it without giving you any pain and perhaps… a bit of pleasure."

Searing heat swamped her from the neck up until she figured her head would burst into flames any moment.

"No… it's not that." His expression grew serious. "All I remember is I was in the midst of a battle and I was thinking I needed to get to Teagan. Next thing I knew, there was a huge explosion. I woke up in the hospital. Teagan was there, trying to get me to the head of the line as far as seeing doctors went. I remember my skin was on fire, the pain was unbearable, and he finally found someone to give me morphine." He looked away. "But morphine only takes away the pain. It doesn't heal the burns…" He sighed, a heavy sound that tugged at her heart. "Burns don't heal like a bruise or a cut. You see, when my skin healed it healed as a series of scars, mostly all over my back. I don't want to scare you by having you ever look at them. I also have some scarring on my chest, and my leg aches something fierce when it's damp."

He stood before she could put a comforting hand on him. "Quinn, it won't matter, really it won't."

"I know you believe that, but… it's not a pretty sight. It's hideous, and I fe—" He shook his head. "You'll turn away from me. You won't be able to stop yourself. Just think about it. I don't want to go any further without you knowing what you might have to look at. I'll… uh, I'll show them to you, if it's a deciding factor." He turned and gazed at her for a moment, but then he left the room.

"Well," she whispered. That was certainly a very different conversation than what she thought he'd have to say. She'd hoped he'd come to tell her that Alicia was leaving, but apparently no such luck there. Poor Quinn, what a burden he carried with him everywhere. She'd seen burn scars before, and they did look bad, but they weren't horrible, and they could never make her turn away. She'd known something was bothering him, but she hadn't been able to figure out what it was. This must be it.

How was she going to convince him it wouldn't bother her? Wouldn't be, what had he called it? A deciding factor? Perhaps if she just talked about it as though it didn't matter, he'd realize it truly didn't. She rubbed her temples. A headache was beginning. She missed the way he used to hold her when she was pregnant. She wanted that intimacy back, and the sooner Quinn realized she wasn't going anywhere the better.

She'd have to be careful that she didn't push him away, though. He was under no obligation to marry either her or Alicia. She knew he cared for her great deal, but did he love her? How much of a factor were his scars in his feelings for others? She loved him for the man he was. But part of that man had a streak of stubborn pride, and it must have been hard to tell her. Her heart hurt for him. As she nursed baby Owen and then laid him in his cradle, a tear fell and landed on his little pink cheek. Gently, she brushed it away with her finger. She was going to convince him she didn't care about those scars. She had to.

CHAPTER SIXTEEN

*Q*uinn didn't feel comfortable in his skin anymore. He didn't like the fact that Alicia knew what he looked like. He sure didn't like the fact that Heaven was probably speculating how badly he was scarred and if she'd ever be able to stomach looking at him. If it was up to him, he'd throw up his hands and be done with it. The ranch was big, and no one said he had to stay near the ranch house.

He turned Bandit toward the Maguire property and rode the fence line. He'd hoped to see his brother, Brogan, who had left abruptly months ago. No one in the family had spoken to him since he'd gone, and Quinn didn't like that one bit. It was pure craziness that their father'd had relations with Gemma's mother. When Brogan was born Mr. Maguire had dropped the baby off at the Kavanagh ranch, and their father had forced their mother to take him in as her own. No one had talked about it. In fact, he didn't even remember it until Gemma mentioned her mother's dying words, and then she had found the birth entry in the Kavanagh Bible.

Brogan had left to live on the Maguire land. It had been sitting empty since Gemma had married Teagan, and

113

Gemma had felt he had some right to it. Quinn wasn't sure he would be welcome, so he wouldn't knock on the front door, or even ride up to it. He just hoped to get a glimpse of his brother.

The ride was peaceful, but he quickly realized there was no cattle on the Maguire land. The pastures were filled with beautiful, majestic horses. Quinn smiled. It had always been Brogan's dream to breed horses. He had a real knack for it, and the horses just loved him. Was he happy? Was he lonely? Would he ever come home? A smile twisted his lips. At least they knew where he was.

The itch to leave and ride across the West again rose within Quinn. It wasn't the restlessness or the hurt that had made him leave before. This time it would be pure avoidance.

He turned Bandit again and patted his neck. "Let's go home, boy."

By the time he rode in, he'd made a decision. He needed to take Heaven for a ride and show her the new safe house and he also needed to find out if she was still willing to marry. Alicia would always be Alicia—Lauren, or whatever her name was. Hopefully, she'd move on to another man. Who knew? Possibly she had a string of them.

As he got closer to the barn, he could tell something was wrong. People were scurrying and his brothers all looked upset. He swung down from his horse and handed the reins to one of the men. He quickly went inside the house, hoping it wasn't Heaven.

Dolly met him at the door her eyes were red and she was wringing her hands. "It's Daisy. She has spots all over her, and she's not feeling well at all. We're waiting on the doc to come."

Quinn started for the stairs, and Dolly grabbed his arm. "You can't go near her. We don't know what's wrong with her, and it could be contagious. Though I'm mostly worried about the baby. So far, Tim looks all right, so I'm not sure where she picked it up from."

"Who's taking care of her?"

"Sullivan volunteered. But the poor thing is so fretful, and she wants her mama. Now don't go running into her room; not if you want to be able to see Heaven and the baby afterward."

He just stared at Dolly. What kind of choice was that? He turned and bounded up the stairs and went into Heaven's room. His heart broke for her. Her eyes were red as cherries, and they were filled with stark fear. Tim was hanging onto her looking as frightened as she did.

Quinn sat on the bed and took Heaven into his arms, kissing her cheek as he pulled her closer. Tim wormed his way into the hug and Quinn kissed him on the top of his head. "What happened?"

It took a moment before Heaven spoke. "I was nursing Owen, and the kids asked if they could play outside. Alicia was already out there with Arnold, and Dolly said she'd keep an eye out. So I let them go. Daisy came in complaining of a sore throat, and Dolly put her right to bed and spoon-fed her hot weak tea. Then suddenly she had a rash. I wasn't allowed to go to her. Quinn, it near broke my heart. She cried for me and cried for me and I couldn't get any closer than the doorway. By then we had sent Sullivan out to get Tim, and Tim seem to be just fine."

"How long ago did you send for the doctor?"

"It seems like forever, but to tell you the truth I don't know." She shook her head in helpless despair. "I want to be in there holding my Daisy but I'm needed here to feed Owen. Tim needs me too."

"Tim, go to the doorway where Sullivan is in and tell him I'll switch with him."

Tim looked at both adults with sad eyes and nodded. He scurried off the bed and went on his way.

Quinn kissed Heaven with everything he had. It was a kiss filled with love, passion, and promise. He cupped her face gently and looked into her eyes. "Daisy will be fine, and I'll be there to comfort her. Just remember I love you." He started to get off the bed then turned and kissed her on the cheek. Then he got up and left the room.

He hugged Tim and sent them back onto his mama. Standing at the doorway, he stared at Daisy. His usually exuberant girl was lying dull eyed with her head on her pillow. He had to swallow hard to keep tears at bay.

"Quinn, you don't have to come in here. Heaven will need someone," Sullivan said.

Quinn walked into the room, sat on the bed, and pulled Daisy to him.

She glanced up at him but she didn't smile. "I lub you," she whispered harshly.

"I love you too, my sweet girl. I hear you're not feeling well, but we're working to make you better. The doctor should be here soon. I thought I would just come in and keep you company for a while."

The two men exchanged worried glances.

"I'll go to get cold water and a few cloths. She starting to burn up. Where is that doctor? He should've been here by now." Shaking his head, Sullivan left the room.

Sullivan had been right. Daisy was burning up. She didn't look well at all. Quinn prayed for Daisy's safety and health. Goodness, he loved this little girl.

Sullivan came back in with the water and cloths and a few towels. "Angus is going to see what's going on with the doctor. I told him if he can't find the doctor, there's a woman, lives at the edge of town, who is a healer." He set the water down and handed a cloth to Quinn. The two of them worked hard to keep Daisy's temperature from rising any higher. Quinn wasn't sure they were making a difference.

Daisy had closed her eyes and hadn't opened them again. Quinn could only hope she was sleeping and not dying. He studied the blotches and blisters on her skin. "I've never seen a rash like that before, have you?"

"If she wasn't this sick, I'd say it was poison ivy, but it must be something else. It's strange that Tim didn't get it and I'm fine. I wonder if Arnold is all right."

"Alicia would have been screaming by now if he wasn't."

Sullivan nodded. "You're right about that. She will be going soon, wouldn't she?"

"I'm hoping, but we'll see what happens."

His little girl moaned and stirred but didn't wake up.

"Daisy? Daisy honey can you hear me?" Quinn continued to try to cool her. He heard people running up the steps and he hoped one of them was the doctor.

A pretty woman with dark hair and dark eyes stood up at the doorway. She had on a crisp white apron and she carried a doctor's bag. "I'm Sheila Kelly. I think I could help if you'd let me."

"Yes, yes, anything you could do would be appreciated," Quinn said as he gestured for her to come into the room.

Sheila came in put down her bag and went back to the doorway for the basin of water that Dolly held. Sheila took it and set it down and went back for clean towels and soap.

"Quinn, is it?"

He nodded.

She offered a gentle smile. "I'll need you to move. You can sit with her as soon as I'm done examining her."

He quickly stood and stepped aside, watching as Sheila washed her hands with the soap and water before she touched Daisy.

"She has a fever, and you did well keeping her cool."

Sheila looked at Daisy's body and then readjusted Daisy's clothes. She frowned and a look of confusion crossed her face. "I've been told she was with two other children, and they are fine?"

Sullivan nodded. "Yes, she was outside playing with Tim and Arnold while Arnold's mother watched them."

"Did she drink anything? Did she touch anything? Has Arnold's mother said what happened or when she noticed that Daisy wasn't feeling well?"

Quinn glanced at Sullivan. "I don't think anyone asked her."

"I'll go," Dolly said from the doorway. "I'll be right back."

"Do you think you know what it is?" Quinn asked.

"Oh, I know what it is. I just want to know how she got it. She'll be fine." Sheila shook her head and looked angry. Then she looked at Sullivan. "If you have potatoes, I need you to mash them up into a paste and I'll need a lot of them. Don't cook them they need to be raw. Where's Daisy's mother?"

Heaven raised her hand. "I'm Daisy's mother. You said she will be fine? But her eyes aren't even open."

Sheila went to the door. "You can come on in. It's not contagious. It's poison ivy. A very large amount, and it seems to be targeted. What I'm saying is somebody either took her clothes off and threw her into a bush of poison ivy or had poison ivy and wiped it all over her somehow. That's why I'd like to talk to the adult who was with the children."

Quinn stepped to the door and took Heaven's hand. He pulled her inside the room. Then he set her on the bed and gave her a clean cloth so she could wipe the cooling water on her daughter.

"Quinn, what about me?" Tim asked.

"You were outside with them, correct?" Sheila asked.

Tim nodded.

"Were you playing with any plants outside?"

Tim shook his head. "Me and Arnold were playing tag and Daisy was helping Miss. Alicia with the garden. Miss. Alicia was tickling Daisy with some leaves, and Daisy was laughing and laughing. They did that for long time. Then she put some into Daisy's mouth, but Daisy spit it out and started to cry."

The adults glanced from one to the other. Everyone looked angry. Alicia must've done this on purpose. There wasn't any other explanation. Poison ivy was bad enough if folks just happened to touch it, but to have it spread onto a child's skin? All over her? How could somebody deliberately do something like that?

Heaven burst into tears. "If she had eaten those leaves, she'd be dead right now."

"More than likely, yes. We need to wash her again with soap this time before we put on the potato paste. I'm grateful she fell asleep, or she'd be screaming."

Alicia stood at the door with Arnold. "I heard you were looking for me. Oh, Daisy really is sick, I thought she just wanted attention as usual."

Quinn balled his hands into fists but kept them by his sides. He was trying to stay as calm as he could. "You and Daisy were playing in the garden?"

"Why, yes, she helped me weed it. She seemed to be having fun."

"Did you happen to see any poison ivy around?" Quinn asked trying to keep his eyes from narrowing on her.

"No, there's none near the property that I've ever seen. Why? What's the problem?"

"You do know what it looks like, don't you?" Quinn asked.

"What's this all about?" Alicia crossed her arms in front of her.

Heaven stood and started for the door but Quinn

wrapped his arm around her waist and pulled her back to him. He glared at Alicia and wondered how he could have ever loved someone like her.

Sheila walked over to Alicia and stuck her hand out. Alicia looked horrified and didn't move to shake Sheila's hand.

"I'm Sheila Kelly, and I'm a healer in these parts. I have never seen a child so covered with poison ivy in my life. She has a high fever because of it, and the recovery is going to take weeks. There is a lot of pain and itching plus headaches that go along with this. So, could you explain how she got all the poison ivy under her clothes?"

Alicia looked Sheila up and down and frowned as though she found her lacking. "I don't have to explain anything to you." Alicia stood there as if that was the end of it.

Quinn had to keep himself from growling. He stepped around Heaven and stood next to Sheila. "We know what happened, we know how it happened, we even know you tried to get her to eat poisonous leaves. What I would like to know is why it happened. We've allowed you to live on the ranch rent free. We've been feeding you and your child for weeks and we haven't asked a thing of you not that you'd pitch in to help ever. And you hurt a *child*? What is wrong with you?"

Alicia pointed at Sheila. "She's not a doctor, and she doesn't know what she's doing. She's just saying what she thinks happened. She has no idea if it's poison ivy or if it's the measles. Don't let her fool you."

Quinn stared at Alicia, unable to believe the words coming out of her mouth. The mouth he had spent so much time yearning to kiss. "I want you out of my sight. I never want you near my children again. Do you understand me?"

"*Your* children!" Alicia snorted. "There's a laugh. Come

along, Arnold, we're not welcome here." Alicia turned to walk away.

"You might as well start packing. I will talk to Teagan, and I'm certain he'll agree that you need to go." Quinn turned his back on her and went to Daisy. He sat on one side of her while Heaven sat on the other, both of them washing her gently with soap and water.

Dolly followed Sullivan into the room. He was carrying a great big pot of mashed raw potatoes. "You should have asked if he knew what a potato looked like before you sent him." Dolly chuckled. She put the pot down on the table next to the bed. Then she looked at everyone in the room. "Anyone that is not a girl needs to leave. I have hot water on the stove and a big cake of soap on the counter. Each one of you is going to wash at least three times, do you hear me?"

Tim's eyes widened as he caught Quinn's gaze. "We really aren't going to wash three whole times are we?"

Quinn chuckled. "Heaven, I will be downstairs if you need me. I'll be making sure everyone washes three whole times. I think everyone needs to wash behind their ears for good measure." He heard Tim groan and smiled. He leaned across Daisy and kissed Heaven's lips quickly. "I'll be back soon."

CHAPTER SEVENTEEN

*T*hree weeks later, Heaven bumped up and down in the wagon with Quinn. He said he had a surprise to show her. She gave him a sidelong glance, warmed when she found him watching her. It hadn't been easy nursing Daisy back to health, but Quinn had been at her side the whole time while they juggled the three children. She loved him with everything she had and then some. And she kept waiting and wanting him to ask her to marry him, but he never did.

They approached a newly built cabin hidden in the forest. Her excitement grew. Could it be? Yes, it must be the safe house for the boys. She had known he would keep his promise, but it was very exciting to see. The wagon had barely rolled to a stop before she jumped down.

The door opened and one of the men who used to come to take the children to a safe place stood there. "I was wondering when you'd get around to seeing me," Ollie Jenks teased.

Heaven hugged Ollie. "I'm so glad to see you're here. How's it working out?"

"We were able to get some of the boys before the other men weeded them out."

"That's wonderful! I'm so glad."

"You can thank your husband. He even sends some of his men over to help."

She didn't bother to correct Ollie's assumption that Quinn and she were married. It was too long of a story why they weren't, and she didn't feel like going into it. "The boys are finding the place easily?"

"Quinn here has had some great ideas about communicating between safe houses and to the boys," Ollie explained. "We're getting more than we ever did, and I'm confident that very few are getting lost."

She turned towards Quinn. "Thank you, you have done so much for me."

Quinn gave her a wide grin. "My pleasure, my love."

They stayed and had coffee. She'd never had a chance to get to know Ollie. The handoff of the children was usually very tense and very quick. It was pleasing to find him to be such a kind, caring, intelligent man. The house was stocked to the brim with supplies and the rooms had actual beds in them. She couldn't have been more pleased.

"Well, Ollie, it's been good to see you," Quinn said as he stood.

He smiled warmly. "Stop by anytime. It's always good to have company."

Heaven stood and went to Ollie giving him a kiss on his cheek. His face turned a fiery crimson, but he smiled. Quinn held out his hand, and Heaven took it, following him to the wagon outside. He helped her up before he jumped to his seat, and then they were off.

"Has anybody heard anything from Alicia?" She gritted her teeth as she said the words, wondering why she'd even asked.

"She's working for Dr. Bright. And she goes by Lauren, which I think is her real name. I don't care as long as she's not bothering us. It was a cruel thing she did to Daisy, and I don't think I can ever forgive her for it." He was trembling as he spoke, and it was reflected in his voice. "I was glad that Teagan was willing to take care of it for us. It was probably fortunate for her as well because I could have strangled her."

"You know," Heaven reasoned. "She never admitted what she did."

"Tim's account was enough for me. I believe him."

"Did—did you ever find out what she was running from?"

"I'm not sure any of the stories she's told are real. My best guess is she was hiding from an overbearing father. She was using a fake name from the start, and she was pretty young then, but now I don't know for sure, although I am starting to believe there's a husband involved."

Heaven turned her head quickly and stared at him. "What do you mean there's a husband involved? She wanted you to marry her," Heaven said in disgust.

"It would've been another name change for her if I had married her." He shook his head as he urged the horses up a low incline. "It's all speculation, but I have a hard time believing she would carry a man's child if she wasn't married to him. She's too calculating for that. Maybe her husband didn't live up to her expectations. I'm still trying to reason out what happened at the hospital. She gave me a couple different stories about that. In one, she said her father wouldn't allow her to stay and in another she said a doctor saw the way she looked at me and transferred her somewhere else. Now, though, I think she realized I had money after Teagan made a sizable donation to the hospital. Who knows? Maybe she was being courted by the doctor and he didn't like her spending time with me." He twisted in his seat and met her gaze. "I do think she's running from someone again."

"She's a strange one, and she cannot be trusted," said Heaven with a shudder. "I never want to see her again. I'm afraid of what I'd do to her. I know the Christian thing to do would be to forgive her, but it's hard to forgive when you don't have all the answers. And she hurt—" She choked back tears. "She hurt my child. I've prayed on this for a while and the furthest I can get is to not hate her." Heaven glanced away. It had taken a lot for her to admit that she didn't hate, but she had reasoned that hating never got her anywhere. She'd work on her forgiveness but when someone tries to kill your child, it was hard very hard. She should've gone to jail.

Quinn turned the wagon onto the road heading toward town. He grinned and patted his front shirt pocket. "Dolly gave me a list of supplies she needed."

"I haven't been to a store in a while. I'm looking forward to exploring new places. And I know two little ones who would love peppermint sticks." She tempered the excitement she felt at getting to town. "But I can't be away too long, Owen will need to be fed soon."

"It shouldn't take long at all. It's just the basics, and on the plus side we get to spend more time together." He put the reins in one hand and settled his other hand over hers.

It never failed to surprise her when she felt the spark between them. It happened every time they touched. Tim would refer to it as mushy. When he grew to be a man hope- fully he would understand it was much, much more.

Quinn slowly released her. He needed both hands on the reins as he drove into town and pulled up in front of the general store. He jumped down and then lifted her from wagon and put her on the boardwalk. They walked into the store together. She loved hearing the bells above the door ring as they entered. They sounded so similar to the store where she had shopped when she'd first been married. All her years of living with her husband, she had hardly ever gone to the store, but when she had, it was the bells that had enchanted her the most, like a jingling, tinkling greeting, so friendly and familiar.

She followed Quinn as he went to the back of the building and greeted the store owner.

"John O'Rourke, this is my wife Heaven." Quinn looked proud when he introduced her.

"My pleasure, ma'am. You got yourself a good one in Quinn." John nodded his balding head and smiled. She had thought Quinn to be very tall, but John O'Rourke was about a foot taller.

Heaven smiled and nodded while her emotions rolled inside of her. Quinn was still pretending to be married and it hurt because he had not made it real. If he wanted to be married all he had to do was ask. Dread filled her stomach, and she began to feel nauseous. She hadn't been looking at what was right in front of her. Rather she only saw what she wanted to see, and she had wanted to see he cared for her. Every breath she took caused her pain in her chest as she stood behind Quinn, smiling.

"Oh, and John could you add three peppermint sticks to the order."

"Will do."

She could feel the heat of Quinn's stare, but she couldn't bring herself look at him.

"You look pale." He touched her on the arm. "Are you feeling all right?"

"I just need some air. I'll be right out front." She quickly walked to the door, and this time she wasn't so enchanted with the sound of the bells ringing.

She didn't know what to think. She didn't know what to

do. She'd been living in a fairytale world she had created. Now that her eyes were open it hurt and hurt bad. She sat down on a bench close to the entrance to the store and closed her eyes for a moment. When she opened them the one person she didn't want to see was bustling toward her.

Alicia was very well-dressed, and her hair was in an elaborate style. She looked healthier now than she had at the ranch.

"I didn't expect to see you so soon. I imagined you still sulking." She stepped way too close to Heaven and glared down at her. "I haven't heard anything about a wedding, or did you two get married in secret?"

Speechless, Heaven stared at the woman. Hadn't she caused enough trouble? Why would she just leave them all alone?

Suddenly Alicia put her hand to her mouth in feigned surprise. "Oh, I shouldn't have said a word to you. I'm sorry. And I'm sorry you're struggling so with the scars on his back, but the truth is the truth, and it's so horrid."

Confusion clouded Heaven's mind. What on earth was this woman talking about?

"Every time I saw him, I thought I would be sick, but as a nurse I had to learn to look past it. Maybe you could just lie there and not touch him. Having the lights off will be a must, I suppose. There is nothing as ugly as those scars on his back, but you can just limit when you have to see them. I *am* sorry for you, though." Alicia looked past her and suddenly turned around and hurried off.

Heaven knew who was behind her. She could feel his heat, and she also knew he must've heard everything Alicia had said. It must have sounded as though she and Alicia had been freely discussing his scars, maybe that they had talked about them many times. She turned and tilted her head back, gazing at him, and she flinched at the cold hard stare he gave her. She quickly looked away. What could she say? And even if she found the words, this wasn't the place to say them.

"Everything is loaded into the wagon. We might as well get going so you can nurse your son." He walked away without waiting for her.

Your son? She wanted to cry; actually she wanted to break down and sob, but she had too much pride. Heaven stood with her head up and her shoulders back and walked to the wagon. Quinn was already sitting on the bench without even waiting to offer her any assistance climbing aboard. She'd been used to doing for herself for years, and she easily climbed up onto the wagon seat.

His face was set in a hard look she'd never seen before. They drove out of town to the ranch without a word being said. He must think he was the only one hurting, but she was hurting too. It was if he suddenly thought his back would be a problem. So, what was his reasoning for not asking her to marry him weeks before? Did he think she had nowhere else to go and he didn't have to marry her? She couldn't be around him she just couldn't. She hopped down and ran inside and then up the stairs.

She tried to relax so she could feed Owen. Daisy and Tim ran up the stairs and sat on the bed with her asking all sorts of questions. She answered them as patiently and cheerfully as she could, and they always seemed to think of just one more. After she burped Owen, she set him back into his cradle where he immediately fell asleep. Now what? She needed to be alone, but she had children. Mothers didn't get the luxury of much time alone.

Dolly knocked on the door and walked in. Their gazes met, and she immediately offered to show Tim and Daisy how to make cookies. After she shooed the children out the door, she followed and closed it behind her.

Heaven stood and looked out the window as tears ran

down her face. Love didn't matter. It didn't matter one bit, at least not where Quinn was concerned. Alicia had accomplished what she had set out to do and that was to break up the bond Heaven and Quinn had formed. She looked down at her left hand and slowly took off the wedding band Sullivan had given her to wear. She put it on the dresser, thinking it would make her feel better but it only made it worse.

She wouldn't be surprised if Quinn rode out and never came back. And his family would blame her for his leaving. Finally, she had caught a glimpse of the loner he could be. He probably had made plans before he ended up at her ranch. She never asked, and he never said. She should've known better than to fall for a man. Quinn had been so unlike her husband, and she had taken his every glance, every touch, so personally and into her heart.

And Quinn had only acted as any polite man should act. It had been her husband who had been cold, often withholding any affection or nice words. She'd wanted to believe everything, and she'd wanted to think she was special, but in actuality she wasn't. She supposed she should've asked Quinn about marriage plans weeks ago. Maybe somewhere in the back of her mind she knew he would never marry her, and she had been unwilling to give up the fantasy. She wasn't good enough for him. Who in their right mind wanted to take on two children plus a baby that was part Indian?

Her poor babies, they were going to be so hurt. She lay on the bed and sobbed into a pillow.

CHAPTER EIGHTEEN

Quinn kicked the fence post and moaned. It hurt more than he could have expected. He had been fooled—again. Heaven had tricked him. She'd made him believe she saw him as a whole man, and she didn't care about his scars. How it hurt to hear Alicia giving her advice on how to avoid touching or seeing his back. The house he was having built for them was almost finished, and he had planned to ask her to marry him for real this time. It would be lonely living in the house but that was what he'd do. Anything to get away from Teagan's happy household.

It was his fault! It was *all* his fault. He had let his guard down, and his heart was mangled once again. He'd sworn never to let another woman into his life or into his heart, and he had stupidly allowed both to happen. Where did they go from here? Heaven was strong enough now after the birth of Owen to strike out on her own. He had no doubt she'd leave. She'd probably had planned to do that all along.

He wished he could hate her, he wished he could put her out of his mind, and he wished most of all that he had never met her. Maybe she could live in the foreman's house for now. He just couldn't stand it, having her and the children in the house with him. He loved those children, and he knew they loved him, but they were young enough to forget him. He looked over at the house and rubbed his chest where his heart pained so much. Who was he kidding? He'd have to leave for a while again. He wouldn't be able to take pity or sympathy from his brothers.

He went into the barn and saddled Bandit. All the supplies he needed were already in the barn. He filled his saddlebags and grabbed his bedroll before he headed out. He didn't stop to say goodbye or to tell anyone of his plans. They'd figure it out soon enough.

CHAPTER NINETEEN

*I*t had been two weeks since Quinn had left. Heaven had arranged for the sale of her ranch, and with the money, outfitted a wagon. She was joining a wagon train, and she had hired two men to help her. Her group was set to leave the next day.

It had been a lonely two weeks during which every thought had been of Quinn. He could have at least said good-bye. It just proved that she was right, and he didn't care. Teagan had tried to talk her into staying and so had Gemma and Dolly, but she just couldn't. This was Quinn's home, not hers.

It had been almost impossible to console Daisy and Tim. They still thought of Quinn as their father. It hadn't been easy to find two trustworthy men to work for her who hadn't balked at Owen being a half breed. Most likely because he was just a baby the two agreed. It was going to be hard to say goodbye to all the people on the ranch; they had all been more than generous and kind to her and her children.

It would be a long difficult trip, but she knew she was up

for it. She had to be she didn't have a choice. But a new start in California was what she needed. She needed time to heal her broken heart and learn to go on with her life. It was amazing at how quickly one's life could change. She had wanted to talk to the local pastor before she left, but she didn't dare go back into town. Instead, she had many talks with the Lord, and she felt He would keep her safe on her journey. She also prayed for Quinn. He deserved a good life. She hoped that once she was gone, he would feel comfortable enough to come home.

Dolly had wanted to set up a special dinner for them, but Heaven couldn't bring herself to take her up on her offer. She'd caused nothing but trouble since she'd arrived. The greatest relief would be not seeing the pity and sorrow in the Kavanaghs' eyes.

Heaven and the children ate their supper in her room that evening, and she woke them up extra early the next morning. She was gone before she had to say goodbye. They probably thought horribly of her, but it was the best she could do.

She drove to the meeting place just outside of town and parked her wagon where the captain directed. Thank goodness, her two hired men showed up on time, and the children seemed excited. She couldn't help but think she was leaving a big part of her heart behind, but there was no help for it.

They spent the day learning the rules of traveling in a group. They practiced circling the wagons, and the captain and his scouts went from wagon to wagon checking to see if they were lightly packed and that everyone had what they needed.

Captain Todd seemed like a fine man, and the two men she had hired, Herman Loud and Jack Vine, were both very respectful. She and her children would be in good hands, and for that she was grateful.

It took a while to get Tim and Daisy settled down for the

night, but finally they were all asleep, including Owen. She looked up at the stars and wondered where she'd gone wrong. Had she been fanciful or had Quinn really loved her? Either way what they'd found had obviously been too fragile, and her heart was still broken into too many pieces to count.

She snuggled against the children and fell asleep.

———

QUINN URGED Bandit to go faster. They had three days on him, but with wagons they'd be going slow. He expected to catch up at any time. His heart ached worse than ever, and he needed to talk to her. He needed to know, was it his back or had he done something else?

He didn't think this wagon train would ever make it up over the mountains before winter set in. They had left too late in the season. It was too dangerous for Heaven and the children. He couldn't wait to see Tim, Daisy, and Owen. He was nervous about seeing Heaven. She wouldn't be happy he had followed them. This time he wasn't going to let the woman he loved just leave without saying goodbye.

"They've stopped for the night, Bandit. We'll catch up soon."

He slowed Bandit to walk as he approached the camp. He looked for guards but didn't see any. He found the captain and explained why he was there, and the captain gave him leave to find Heaven.

It didn't take him but a minute to find them. Daisy and Tim were running around while Heaven was bending over the fire stirring their supper. He walked over and Daisy and Tim came to a halt. They looked at each other, and when he kneeled on the ground they ran into his arms.

"Where have you been? All mama does is cry!" Tim asked with narrowed eyes.

"Why did you go away, Dada? I lub you very very very very very much." Daisy kissed his cheek every time she said very.

His heart was near exploding with love for these two. He glanced up and found Heaven staring at him. There was no emotion on her face, and that scared him. He gave her his best grin, stood, and walked toward her. He locked his gaze with hers and was pleased when she finally smiled. He opened his arms, and she flew into them as she gave a little cry. He held her close, not wanting to let her go again.

"I can't believe you're here. Quinn, why did you come?"

He pulled her closer and whispered into her ear, "Because I love you."

She pulled back and stared into his eyes. "You what? But you left."

He nodded, awash in shame. "I was so wrapped up in my own hurt that I didn't think about your feelings. I still don't know how you feel or what you want. I heard all the advice you asked Alicia for and just couldn't stay. Not after building us a house. I couldn't face living in it alone. I wanted us to be a family…"

"I never asked for her advice." Heaven drew back and locked onto his gaze. "That was her way of trying to make trouble. Quinn, I don't care what your back looks like. I wouldn't care if you had scars all over your body except for the pain I know that would be. I love you too. I've been so torn up and I couldn't stay. Everything reminded me of you, and I just couldn't take it." Tears filled her eyes.

Before he could say anything, he was ambushed by Tim and Daisy hugging him. Being loved was the best thing in the world.

atching Quinn with the children was the best thing for her. He lay on his back, napping with Owen on his chest. They both had the slightest snore. Quinn found another family who would take on Henry Loud and Jack Vine so they could still make the trip west. He paid half their wages with the promise to pay the rest when they arrived in California. He planned to drive the wagon back to the ranch, though he still didn't mention getting married.

It turned out to be a very cramped way to sleep. Daisy insisted that Dada sleep in the wagon with them. Heaven had Owen in his cradle above her head, and Quinn had both Tim and Daisy sprawled across him. She couldn't help but giggle when one of the children moved or turned. It wasn't comfortable, but her heart no longer hurt.

On their third day riding back, Quinn drove them into town, and she felt ill. Everyone would know by now they never were married. He stopped right in front of the preacher's house and hurried them all inside. And just like that, before she knew it, she was Mrs. Quinn Kavanagh. She barely looked at the ring until they were on the way to the ranch. When she did glance down at her hand, she was stunned. It was a different ring.

"Look at the engraving."

She slid the ring off and found one word engraved on the inside: *Forever*. Her eyes watered. "How long have you had this ring?"

"I bought it a few days after we moved onto the ranch. I wanted the house built first, and then…" His face took on a sheepish expression.

A smile tugged at her lips and she touched him on the arm. "I had my moments of doubt too, but we are finally married," she told him.

"Forever," he whispered.

"Forever," she whispered back.

EPILOGUE

*S*he'd been right to keep her faith. God had opened the most wonderful door for her and the children. When she saw the scars, they didn't seem ugly, but they did make her want to cry. He must have suffered horribly. Quinn showed her what love, gentleness and affection could be.

"What are you thinking about?" she asked.

"I was wondering which brother would sacrifice himself." His lips twitched. He took her hand and led her off the porch so they could see the stars.

"The more wives the merrier if that was what you meant by sacrifice," she teased back. Then she grew serious. "Was it a sacrifice to marry me?"

"Loving you has been the biggest risk of my life and I'm the happiest of men that I took that risk." He gathered her into his arms and kissed her.

"To answer your question, I think I'd need to meet your brother, Brogan before I could give the best guess."

Quinn nodded. "He's been on his own long enough. I'll go over to the Maguire ranch and check on him. Meanwhile we should look around for a wife for Sullivan. Like you said the more the merrier."

"I love you Quinn."

"That's good because I love you too."

ABOUT THE AUTHOR

Sexy Cowboys and the Women Who Love Them...
Finalist in the 2012 and 2015 RONE Awards.
Top Pick, Five Star Series from the Romance Review.
Kathleen Ball writes contemporary and historical western
romance with great emotion and
memorable characters. Her books are award winners and
have appeared on best sellers lists including: Amazon's Best
Seller's List, All Romance Ebooks, Bookstrand, Desert
Breeze Publishing and Secret Cravings Publishing Best
Sellers list. She is the recipient of eight Editor's Choice
Awards, and The Readers' Choice Award for Ryelee's
Cowboy.
Winner of the Lear diamond award Best Historical Novel-
Cinders' Bride
There's something about a cowboy

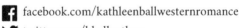

facebook.com/kathleenballwesternromance
twitter.com/kballauthor
instagram.com/author_kathleenball

OTHER BOOKS BY KATHLEEN

Lasso Spring Series

Callie's Heart

Lone Star Joy

Stetson's Storm

Dawson Ranch Series

Texas Haven

Ryelee's Cowboy

Cowboy Season Series

Summer's Desire

Autumn's Hope

Winter's Embrace

Spring's Delight

Mail Order Brides of Texas

Cinder's Bride

Keegan's Bride

Shane's Bride

Tramp's Bride

Poor Boy's Christmas

Oregon Trail Dreamin'

We've Only Just Begun

A Lifetime to Share

A Love Worth Searching For

So Many Roads to Choose

The Settlers

Greg

Juan

Scarlett

Mail Order Brides of Spring Water

Tattered Hearts

Shattered Trust

Glory's Groom

Battered Soul

Romance on the Oregon Trail

Cora's Courage

Luella's Longing

Dawn's Destiny

Terra's Trial

Candle Glow and Mistletoe

The Kabvanagh Brothers

Teagan: Cowboy Strong

Quinn: Cowboy Risk

Brogan: Cowboy Pride

The Greatest Gift

Love So Deep

Luke's Fate

Whispered Love

Love Before Midnight

I'm Forever Yours

Finn's Fortune

Glory's Groom

Made in the USA
Coppell, TX
13 February 2021